P9-DND-556

He'd give her the truth—whether she could handle it or not

"The least you could do is come up with a good story," Levi snapped, eyes blazing, before he could speak.

Seth hit the brakes, but it wasn't until the car stopped that he looked over at her. She had the handcuffed hand braced against the seat, and she looked at him like he were a madman.

"You don't get it, do you?" he ground out. "I don't have to come up with any story. I was hired to bring you here. Let's not kid ourselves. Someone took care of your bodyguards, someone blew up the cabin. I may be going out on a limb here but I think we were supposed to be inside it."

"What are you saying?" She swallowed hard.

"That someone knows too much about you and me. Someone who wants us both dead.'

"That's ridiculous. I might have been kidnapped for money, but kill me? Why?" When he shook his head, she went on. "Don't you know anything?"

"I might not be the knight in shining armor you hoped for, princess, but I'm all you've got."

"What if I preferred to save myself instead of—"

He cut her off. "You wouldn't last twenty-four hours on your own."

Her eyes narrowed and pierced his. "How do I know I'll last twenty-four hours with *you*?"

Dear Reader,

When actions of the past come home to haunt Senator James Marshall McCord, Texas rancher and recipient of the Congressional Medal of Honor, he knows he must protect the people he loves most in the world—his family. But he'll need some help from three very rugged, very determined men.

Harlequin Intrigue is proud to bring together three of your favorite authors in a *new* miniseries: THE McCORD FAMILY COUNTDOWN.

Starting in October get swept away by a mysterious bodyguard in #533 *Stolen Moments* by B.J. Daniels. Then meet the sexy town sheriff in #537 *Memories at Midnight* by Joanna Wayne. And finally, feel safe in the strong arms of a tough city cop in #541 *Each Precious Hour* by Gayle Wilson.

In a race against time, only love can save them. Don't miss a minute!

Enjoy,

Denise O'Sullivan
Associate Senior Editor
Harlequin Books
300 East 42nd Street
New York, NY 10017

Stolen Moments
B.J. Daniels

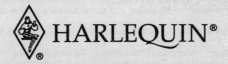

HARLEQUIN®

TORONTO • NEW YORK • LONDON
AMSTERDAM • PARIS • SYDNEY • HAMBURG
STOCKHOLM • ATHENS • TOKYO • MILAN • MADRID
PRAGUE • WARSAW • BUDAPEST • AUCKLAND

If you purchased this book without a cover you should be aware
that this book is stolen property. It was reported as "unsold and
destroyed" to the publisher, and neither the author nor the
publisher has received any payment for this "stripped book."

ISBN 0-373-22533-4

STOLEN MOMENTS

Copyright © 1999 by Barbara Heinlein

All rights reserved. Except for use in any review, the reproduction or
utilization of this work in whole or in part in any form by any electronic,
mechanical or other means, now known or hereafter invented, including
xerography, photocopying and recording, or in any information storage
or retrieval system, is forbidden without the written permission of the
publisher, Harlequin Enterprises Limited, 225 Duncan Mill Road,
Don Mills, Ontario, Canada M3B 3K9.

All characters in this book have no existence outside the imagination of
the author and have no relation whatsoever to anyone bearing the same
name or names. They are not even distantly inspired by any individual
known or unknown to the author, and all incidents are pure invention.

This edition published by arrangement with Harlequin Books S.A.

® and TM are trademarks of the publisher. Trademarks indicated with
® are registered in the United States Patent and Trademark Office, the
Canadian Trade Marks Office and in other countries.

Visit us at www.romance.net

Printed in U.S.A.

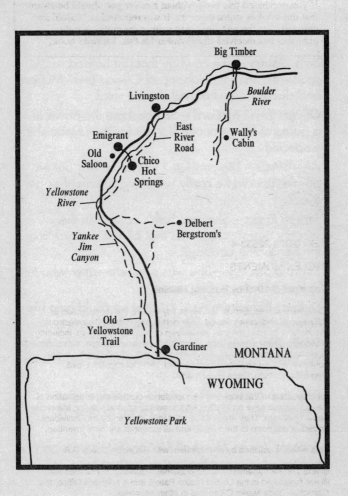

Big Timber

Livingston

Boulder River

Emigrant

East River Road

Wally's Cabin

Old Saloon

Chico Hot Springs

Yellowstone River

Delbert Bergstrom's

Yankee Jim Canyon

Old Yellowstone Trail

Gardiner

MONTANA

WYOMING

Yellowstone Park

CAST OF CHARACTERS

Seth Gantry — The cowboy thought he had problems. Then he kidnapped Olivia "Levi" McCord and discovered what real trouble was!

Olivia "Levi" McCord — She became the pawn in a game of life or death, but not for the reason she suspected.

Alex Wells — The convicted murderer was out on parole. But did he really want to go straight or get even?

Jerilyn Ryers — She was Seth's partner in the security business, but was that all she wanted from the handsome cowboy?

Shanna Stanley — She was a heartbreaker who fell in love with the wrong man.

Delbert Bergstrom — He thought he could help his nephew start a new life. He was dead wrong.

Wally Stanley — He was the only person who knew the truth — but someone was determined he'd never tell.

Billy Bob Larson — He carried a grudge since Vietnam, but how far would he go to destroy McCord?

Senator James Marshall McCord — His passion was politics — but not at the cost of his family.

ABOUT THE AUTHOR

B.J. Daniels lives in Livingston, Montana, one of the windiest places on earth. But just like her heroine in *Stolen Moments*, B.J. believes home is where the heart is, regardless of the weather. And both B.J. and her heroine's heart reside in Montana with the men they love.

B.J. loves to hear from readers. Write to her at: P.O. Box 183, Bozeman, MT 59771.

Books by B.J. Daniels

HARLEQUIN INTRIGUE
312—ODD MAN OUT
353—OUTLAWED!
417—HOTSHOT P.I.
446—UNDERCOVER CHRISTMAS
493—A FATHER FOR HER BABY

Don't miss any of our special offers. Write to us at the following address for information on our newest releases.

Harlequin Reader Service
U.S.: 3010 Walden Ave., P.O. Box 1325, Buffalo, NY 14269Canadian: P.O. Box 609, Fort Erie, Ont. L2A 5X3

This book is humbly dedicated to my friends
Chris and Lise who opened their arms and their
home to me, fed me better than I deserve and always
have a cold Diet Coke waiting for me.
Thanks for always being there.

Chapter One

Thanksgiving Day
Thursday, November 25, 1999

"Olivia? *Olivia?*"

"Levi!" Natalie whispered beside her.

With a start, Levi glanced up from her plate to see her friend Natalie making eye motions toward the head of the table. Levi shifted her gaze to find her father standing, wineglass in hand, waiting patiently. And she realized he'd been calling her name. Her given name.

For the second time that afternoon, James Marshall McCord had her worried. He never called her Olivia. She'd been Levi since infancy, leaving little doubt how much he'd hoped for a son. But she'd never minded. She liked "Levi." It fit the tomboy she'd been, the ranch woman she'd become. It fit her in a way she suspected "Olivia" never would.

"Levi?" he asked, smiling down the table at her. "Are you all right?"

That was exactly what she wanted to ask *him*. She met his gaze and saw something flicker in his blue eyes. *He'd lied.* And he knew that she knew it.

"I'm sorry, Daddy," she said, brushing a tendril of hair back from her face. Her hair was long and dark, a wild mane of loose waves that fell to the middle of her back. Unlike her father's once pale blond, straight hair. His blond had changed to white over the years, making him look even more distinguished. Levi, she was told, had taken after her mother in not only her looks and hair, but her strong-willed temperament.

"I'm sorry," she said. "I'm afraid I wasn't listening."

James Marshall laughed, his gaze lingering affectionately on her for a long moment. "It's all right, Levi. I know how politics bores you and lately that's all we've talked about. *I'm* the one who's sorry."

Levi felt like the traitor she was. She didn't just dislike politics, she hated it and she wished her father did, as well. She knew she was being selfish. Why couldn't she be more like her cousin Robin, who not only wholeheartedly supported Senator James Marshall McCord's political rise, but worked as his aide? Or even her friend Natalie, who at least took an interest.

But as Levi looked down the table at her father, it startled her to think that this larger-than-life handsome man with the deep blue eyes and an abundance of Texas charm could be the next president of the United States. And according to the polls, he had a good chance once he threw his hat into the ring. *If* he threw his hat into the ring.

"I was about to make a toast," James Marshall said, his voice soft, his gaze warm as it moved around the table from Mary, who had always been more like family than their cook, to his top advisor

Whitt Emory, to his niece and aide Robin, to Levi's closest friend, Natalie.

He raised his wineglass. "You have all made this day very special by being here on the Altamira. I am very thankful to have you in my life." His gaze stopped on Levi. "To Texas and all of you. Happy Thanksgiving!"

Levi lifted her glass without taking her eyes away from her father's face. She took a sip of her wine, not even tasting it. She replayed the conversation she'd overheard between Sheriff Clint Richards and her father again, trying to convince herself that she'd just imagined he'd lied to the sheriff earlier.

"I got your message," Clint had said to the senator. Both men had had their backs to her, neither aware of her presence just inside the den doorway. "I came right out."

"Thanks, Clint, I—I'm sorry I bothered you, especially on Thanksgiving."

"You made it sound urgent," the sheriff said.

"One of the hands thought he'd found a place where some fence had been cut," her father said. "But it doesn't look like any cattle are missing or any real damage done."

"You're sure that's all it was?" Clint sounded surprised.

Her father nodded. "I feel foolish for calling you. Especially today."

"No problem. I'll keep a lookout."

That was when her father had turned to see her standing in the doorway. It was more than his startled expression. More than the fact that this was the first time Levi had heard about a cut fence. More than the mutual knowledge that the senator hadn't been involved in running the ranch since he'd gotten into politics, years before. They both knew the ranch foreman, Freddie Caulder, wouldn't have gone to him with the problem; he would have come to her.

Her father was lying. There was no cut fence. She could see it in his expression. Feel it in her heart. Nor would her father call Clint out on Thanksgiving over a cut fence.

James Marshall dropped his gaze from her. "Can you stay for Thanksgiving dinner?" he had asked Clint.

Levi had stepped away, shocked. She knew her father wouldn't lie to Clint unless he had a good reason. So why had he really called the sheriff?

Clint politely declined dinner, saying he already had plans. She watched the sheriff leave, intending to have a word alone with her father.

But then Whitt had arrived, followed close behind by Robin and Natalie. A few minutes later, dinner was served.

"I was just telling Robin that the three of us should go on a vacation," her father said now.

A vacation? Now? She glanced over at her cousin. Robin looked as surprised as Levi.

"I'm not sure that would be a good idea, Senator." Whitt spoke up, but no one seemed to be paying any attention to him.

Had her father changed his mind about running for president? Levi felt a surge of hope, then stopped herself. When James Marshall set his mind to something, nothing could deter him. He loved politics and believed he could make a difference. She knew he'd make a fine president. But she did wonder why he hadn't declared his candidacy yet. What was holding him back? Was he having second thoughts? Did she dare hope?

"You *are* still planning to announce your candidacy for president?" she asked, her heart in her throat.

"Of course he's going to run," Robin said, sounding so proud of him that Levi felt herself flush with guilt.

"I just thought we could get away for a few days before…before all the craziness really begins," her father said.

He *was* going to run, she thought. That was why he suggested a vacation now, before the holidays, before he declared, because who knew when they'd have time together after that.

"This just doesn't seem like the time for you to leave, Jim," Whitt said.

"Whitt's right, Uncle Jim," Robin echoed. "There is so much to be done. But it was a nice idea. Remember when the three of us went to Big Bend National Park?" That was right after Robin had come to live with them, not long after her father had been killed.

Levi felt her father's gaze on her and looked up to meet it. Did his reason for lying to Sheriff Richards have anything to do with this sudden vacation for the three of them?

"You're right, of course, Whitt. You too, Robin." Her father looked disappointed. Or was it worried?

She stared at him, her mouth dry and her eyes burning. What was going on? Something. And damned if she wasn't going to find out. Right after dinner was over, Thanksgiving or not.

Mary served pumpkin pie with whipped cream, offering her two cents worth as she joined them again at the table.

The short, plump redheaded cook had been with

the McCord family since before Levi was born. Catherine Olivia McCord had died when Levi was three. James Marshall had never remarried. Mary had been like a mother to Levi, and later to Robin.

"You have to announce your candidacy before the New Year," Mary said with authority. "Give the people of this country something to look forward to in the new millennium."

"If the world doesn't come to an end," Whitt offered with a laugh.

The conversation around the table went quickly back to politics and when the senator should declare. Levi pushed pie around on her plate, feeling a distance that frightened her.

"Daddy, I need to talk to you," she said the moment the meal was finally over.

"Sure, sweetheart." The phone rang. He frowned. "Oh, Levi, I forgot, Whitt and Robin and I are expecting a conference call," he apologized. "Can it wait until later?"

Levi started to say "No." Something inside her feared it couldn't wait, but she told herself she was being silly.

"Sure. I'm going to give Natalie a ride home," she said, touching her father's broad shoulder, feeling a strength that reassured her. "I won't be long."

He smiled and covered her small hand with his large one as he gazed down at her. His eyes suddenly shimmered and, quite without warning, he pulled her into his arms and hugged her tightly. "Trust me, Levi, everything's going to be all right," he whispered so softly she was afraid she hadn't heard him right. "I love you. Remember that always."

She clung to him, more afraid than ever. "Daddy—"

He pulled back. Whitt called from down the hall to say they were waiting for him. "I have to go." He gave her a reassuring smile. "Drive carefully. No, drive skillfully," he said over his shoulder as he strode down the hall.

Levi watched him go. Although James Marshall wore a prosthesis in place of the leg he'd lost in Vietnam, he seldom let it show in his gait. Only when he was tired or upset did he limp. He was limping now, she noted.

He stopped at the doorway to his den and turned to look back at her. "Great to see you again, Natalie. Sorry to hear your car broke down, though."

Levi watched him disappear into the room and close the door behind him as she fought the ridiculous feeling that she might never see him again.

"Are you all right?" Natalie asked beside her. "You've been acting weird today."

"I'm worried about Daddy," Levi said, thinking that when she got back to the ranch, she'd check with the foreman about a cut fence before she spoke with her father. She desperately wanted to be wrong. Or at least, if not wrong, get some answers that would make her feel a little less frightened.

"Don't worry, he'll make a great president," Natalie said.

"Yeah?" So why did she feel that might not happen? Was it a premonition? Or just wishful thinking? "What if I don't want to be a president's daughter?"

Natalie slipped her arm around her friend. "Just think of the men who'll want to date you."

They both laughed. It felt good. "You want to call a tow truck for your car before we leave?"

"On Thanksgiving? No way. I'll get it towed tomorrow. Come on, I've been dying all day to tell you about this guy I met at work."

They crossed the wide veranda, the afternoon mild and scented with the fragrances of fall in the Texas Hill Country.

THE MOMENT LEVI PULLED OUT of the ranch road and headed down the two-lane county road that led into San Antonio, she picked up two vehicles tailing behind her instead of the usual one. She watched for a moment in her rearview mirror. Had her father increased her private security?

Levi sped up, then slowed. Both cars stayed the same distance behind her. The increased security could just be a precaution as the time neared for the senator to announce his candidacy for president. Or it could validate all her fears.

"What is it?" Natalie asked, turning to look back.

"Just more big, strong men paid to protect me," Levi said. "Can't wait until I have Secret Service following me everywhere."

"Oh, you'll love all that attention."

"Sure, wait until we double-date." Her father had hired the full-time security guards for her over a year ago, right after he received a death threat at the ranch. While it had turned out to be nothing, he'd kept the security guards on as a precaution. "You hang around me and we'll both be old maids."

"Remember that one time?" Natalie said, laughing. "That really cute bodyguard your father hired?"

Levi only half listened as she checked her rearview mirror again to see that both vehicles were still behind her. She had to admit that normally she resented the intrusion in her life, but today the security guards reassured her. They made her feel everything really might be all right, because she knew others like them were guarding the ranch right now. Guarding her father.

"Can you believe my new car broke down?" Natalie bemoaned as they passed the Mustang convertible parked on the edge of the road. "It's a good thing Robin came along when she did."

"Your car just quit?"

Natalie shrugged. "I told you we should have taken auto mechanics in college."

"Or at least date someone who knows how to fix cars," Levi suggested. "So tell me about this guy you met."

They talked and laughed on the way to Natalie's house, the cool night air blowing in the windows. It wasn't until later, long after Levi was on the county road headed back home, the day dying around her and an approaching thunderstorm darkening the sky, that she happened to glance into her rearview mirror.

Her foot came off the gas. She stared into the mirror, then turned to look out the back window.

There were no car lights behind her. No cars. Nothing but empty road. She was alone. Completely alone.

Panic curled tight fingers around Levi's throat as she stared back at the growing darkness. She swallowed, telling herself there was no cause for concern. But the lie wouldn't go down. She'd lost her security guards. Wasn't that what she'd often wished for? Freedom? Anonymity? What she considered an ordinary life?

She stared at the empty gravel road behind her. Suddenly she had her freedom, but she knew instinctively, this was not what she wanted. Not today.

For a moment, she thought about turning around and going back to look for them. But the thunderstorm was right behind her, moving in fast.

She sped up, watching the road ahead as she picked up the car phone and hurriedly dialed the ranch. Her hand shook as she held the phone against her ear and checked the rearview mirror. Nothing but the storm, the empty back road and the growing darkness.

She'd known for years that there were people who might use her to get to her father, but until tonight she hadn't realized just what that meant, the danger not only to herself but ultimately to her father. She was Senator James Marshall McCord's daughter. His only offspring. The daughter of a possible future president. He'd done everything he could to protect her from publicity and keep her out of the public eye. But being a politician's daughter had always come with a price, none higher than at this moment.

As she waited for the phone to ring, she tried to think of a half-dozen good reasons why the security men weren't behind her. She couldn't come up with even one. They'd been told never to leave her. Never. Under any circumstances. They wouldn't disobey Senator James Marshall McCord. They'd all been handpicked by him personally. So where were they?

It took Levi a moment to realize the phone wasn't ringing. She hurriedly dialed again, thinking she'd missed a number, but halfway through she heard the silence and knew the phone was dead. She shook it, then checked the battery. For a long moment, she stared, uncomprehending, into the empty hole where the battery should have been. Had it fallen out? How could that have happened?

Her fear escalating, she threw down the phone and locked all the car's doors. Ahead, the solitary beams of her headlights cut through the dark late Texas afternoon, making her feel all the more vulnerable.

She pushed down on the gas pedal, gathering speed, gathering courage. She was safe. There was a logical explanation for this. A logical explanation for everything that had happened today. But she knew better. She was alone for the first time since her father's death threat more than a year ago. All alone on an isolated back road, miles from the ranch, miles from town.

Fear mixed with anger. She didn't want this. Any of it. Her father had put his life in danger and hers, as well. Tears of anger blurred her vision.

The car fishtailed around a corner and she slowed, but not much. She knew she was driving too fast. But she felt an urgency to get to the ranch as quickly as possible. Unfortunately, the road ahead was even more narrow and full of curves as it wound through the hills, and the storm was gaining on her.

She careened around another corner and was forced to slow even more for the next one. Ahead she could see Natalie's new car in the barrow ditch where she'd left it earlier.

If the Mustang hadn't broken down, Levi would be at the ranch now. The thought raced past, making her heart race with it. Surely Natalie's car trouble wasn't part of some plot to— To what? To get her out on this road today?

She was telling herself she was just being overly

suspicious when she looked in her rearview mirror again. Instead of the blank darkness, light shone a few miles behind her. One of her security guards?

Suddenly she could think of several scenarios to explain their temporary absence. Maybe one had broken down, like Natalie's car. Just an odd coincidence. Nothing to panic over.

Or maybe there'd been an accident involving one or both of the cars. It didn't matter. She was convinced that at least one of them was with her again. She let out a sigh of relief as she waited for the car to catch her.

But as the vehicle neared, she saw that it wasn't a set of headlights but a solitary light speeding toward her. And the vehicle didn't slow, nor did it drop in behind her. It kept coming, moving faster than she thought necessary or prudent.

Ahead she could see a sharp curve in the road. Behind her, the single light grew larger and larger until it filled her car, blinding her.

At the curve, she belatedly realized she was going too fast. She hit the brakes and the car began to slide around the corner. Behind her, the single headlight stayed on her. But as she came out of the curve, it moved up fast on her left and roared past.

That was when she saw that it wasn't a car at all but a motorcycle. A dark, hooded figure hunched over the bike as it disappeared over the next rise in a cloud of dust and dusky darkness.

Shaken, Levi slowed the car and relaxed her hands on the wheel, keenly aware of the trembling in her fingers, in her legs. She tried to calm herself. She felt idiotic. She'd actually thought the biker had planned to force her off the road. Instead, the fool was probably just trying to outrun the storm.

This wasn't like her. She didn't panic easily, didn't let things spook her. But she was spooked.

Behind her, the road was again empty but darker as the storm swept in. Ahead, the single headlight beam of the motorcycle shone in the distance then disappeared around a bend in the road.

It comforted her a little just knowing she wasn't alone on this back road. The ranch wasn't far now. Another five miles to the turnoff. Then she'd be home. Safe.

Rain began to fall, huge, sopping drops that pelted the windshield like pebbles. Lightning lit the sky for an instant, then thunderclouds obliterated everything like some ominous eclipse.

She turned on the wipers, dropped down a hill and around a sharp curve. Her headlights picked up the stone abutments of the bridge over the creek and something else. Something in the middle of the road at the mouth of the narrow bridge. Something large and bright. The rain-streaked shine of polished chrome turned into a motorcycle. The motorcycle lay on its side in the middle of the road, the rider sprawled next to it, blocking the road.

Levi laid into her brakes, the car skidding through the downpour toward the fallen bike and rider.

The fool, she thought frantically. He'd been going way too fast for the conditions and the storm had still caught him.

She stopped the car just feet from the rider. Her headlights pierced the falling rain to illuminate skid marks in the gravel and mud, the wrecked bike, the motionless rider.

Levi didn't remember rolling down her window as she brought the car to a standstill. But now rain swept in, accompanied by a low, mournful moan.

In the headlights, she saw the rider lift one arm, then let it drop again. As the rider tried to get up, the hood fell back, exposing a head of long red hair and a distinctive female profile. Another moan shattered the stillness.

Levi hesitated, but only for an instant. She realized that the woman could lie there for hours and no one else might come along on this road tonight, especially with it being Thanksgiving.

After opening the car door, Levi got out, the rain drenching her to the skin through the thin cotton of her holiday dress as she started toward the downed biker.

A boot heel crunched on the gravel behind her. Levi started to turn. Out of the corner of her eye, she caught the outline of a large dark figure, but before she could react, strong arms enveloped her, lifting her off her feet. A massive hand muffled her screams as she was dragged backward through the rain.

In the glare of the headlights, she watched the redhead get effortlessly to her feet and turn to look at her. For a fleeting instant, Levi thought she saw surprise in the woman's expression. Then she felt something prick her skin. And everything went black.

Chapter Two

Levi swam in a sea of warm darkness, caught in its seductive hold. She didn't know how long she'd been under as she began to swim toward the surface, sensing the light above her growing brighter.

If only she could open her eyelids, but the effort was too much. Her limbs felt leaden and her mind groggy and jumbled with strange, terrifying images that danced in and out and seemed so real. She tried to grasp one, but it scudded away, a wisp no more tangible than smoke.

Still shrouded in the ominous dreams, she finally managed to surface, opening her eyes a crack, afraid of what she'd find. She blinked, becoming aware of two things. She was in a small airplane—a private jet, by the plush interior and propellerless hum—and she was not alone.

FROM ACROSS THE AISLE, Seth Gantry watched her come out of the drug-induced sleep. The resemblance had been startling. He'd seen it the moment she stepped from her car into the glare of the headlights. Her hair, a tumble of dark burnished waves

cascading around her shoulders. Her body, slim and
long, softened by full curves.

It had stopped him like a shotgun blast to his
chest. Shanna. He'd stood, too stunned to move. For
one breath-stealing moment, he'd believed it really
was her standing there. Then she'd turned and he'd
seen the woman's face. And reality had come like a
blow.

But even now in the light of the plane's interior,
he could see similarities between the two women.
The hair. The wide-set eyes fringed with dark lashes.
The high cheekbones.

But he could also see differences. The full, sensual mouth. The patrician features.

And yet when she opened her eyes, he thought
they would be blue. As blue as Texas bluebonnets.
And as filled with that silent pleading as the last time
he'd looked into them.

The woman opened her eyes, blinked, then looked
over at him. They weren't blue at all, but a surprising pale violet. And all he saw in them was a
drugged blankness.

She wasn't Shanna. Not that he'd really believed
she was. Except for that split second of insanity. So
why did just looking at her hurt so much?

"Hello," he said, his voice rough with emotions
he thought he'd buried years ago. Obviously he
hadn't buried them deep enough. Disappointment sat
on his chest, making each breath a hard-won victory.

She blinked again, looking at him with an empty
vagueness that confirmed the heavy-duty muscle re-
laxant had done its job.

The question was: How much did she remember?
She looked confused and probably incoherent. But

would she experience the usual short-term memory loss?

He hoped so. It would be better if she didn't remember what had happened to her, he thought, absently rubbing his hand where she'd bitten him. Seth liked fight in a woman. Just not *this* woman. And not now.

As he watched her, he remembered the feel of her in his arms—her surprising physical strength, as well as her strength of will. He waited expectantly, still seeing Shanna in her and wishing he didn't.

She offered a drunken lopsided smile. There was no sign of nausea, he thought, pleased with his choice of drugs. Nor any fear in her expression. Yet. He knew it would take a few minutes before she'd be coherent and by then they'd have landed and she wouldn't be his problem anymore. This was one job he'd be glad to have over.

She frowned and looked around, her gaze questioning. He wondered if every emotion this woman felt showed as clearly on her face, or if it was just her drugged, uninhibited state. Again he felt that tug of interest and found himself wondering about her. He caught himself. It didn't matter. Actually, it was better not to know. It made things easier. Less personal. And that's the way he liked them.

"You're in a plane," he said in response to the look. "We'll be landing soon."

The brows unfurrowed. She blinked and seemed to study the plane as if she thought she should recognize it. Why did he get the feeling she'd been in a private jet before? For the moment, she seemed satisfied with his answer and he was glad of that.

When she looked at him again, the violet eyes registered flashes of random emotions from confu-

sion to curiosity. But it was the intelligence he saw
there that worried him. Intelligence *and* strength of
will? Seth hoped he wouldn't regret that he hadn't
handcuffed her to the seat.

SHE WAS FLYING? It didn't surprise her. She felt airborne and wasn't sure she even needed the aircraft.
Her thoughts zipped in and out like fighter planes,
so fast she couldn't catch even one for more than
an instant. Her body floated as if weightless, although it seemed to be slumped in the plush seat.
Her brain was unable to get her limbs to respond.

She smiled to herself, relishing this alien not-
necessarily-unpleasant feeling. If she'd been able to
reason, she'd have been horrified at this inability to
think or move, let alone the idea of waking in a jet
with a strange man. She didn't even like to have
more than a glass of wine because of her need to be
in control at all times.

But *that* Levi was gone. This Levi couldn't care
less. She soared. Free. And it felt…delicious.

While she had no fear of flying, she did wonder
how this cowboy had ended up on her magic carpet
ride. As she looked over at him, she also wondered
who he was and how she felt about him. She had
no idea how she *should* feel about him, since her
mind was still senseless and her body wonderfully
insensible, but she felt *something*. In fact, her aware-
ness of him seemed magnified, as if just one touch,
even one whiff, would tell her everything she
needed to know.

She closed her eyes and sniffed. Mmm. *Very*
male. Unique as fingerprints and just as telling, his
masculine scent seemed to fill her with what she
knew instinctively were small truths about him.

Strong. She smiled as another truth invaded her senses. Sexy. *Very* sexy. She opened her eyes, drunk with the essence of him, and grinned. At least she thought she grinned.

He gave her a small smile. She thought she felt her grin deepen into a smile, but who knew. She liked to think at least her lips were working.

"Would you care for some juice?" he asked.

Nice voice. Soft, considerate and something else that dodged her grasp. Apprehensive? That didn't make any sense. What would he have to be apprehensive about?

She passed on the juice with a laborious shake of her head, feeling too far beyond forming the words "No, thank you."

He didn't seem to mind. Part of her watched him open an orange juice and take a drink.

His hands drew her attention. Large hands. She blinked, still staring at his long, sensuous fingers, as a jolt of fear shot through her. Odd, she thought, dragging her gaze back to his face. Where had that come from?

Nothing about the man looked dangerous. Certainly not his face. It was a pleasing sculpture of strong angles and planes, broken by the midnight black of his thick cowboy mustache that softened the hardness of bone and muscle to make him downright handsome. The mustache filled his upper lip and curled down past the corner of each side of his wide, well-defined mouth. His hair, the same shiny black, was thick and long enough to brush his collar.

Dressed as he was, he could have passed for one of the ranchers who frequented the Cattleman's Club in San Antonio. He wore jeans, a blue-checked western shirt, a leather vest, a tooled leather belt with an elk-horn buckle and western boots. A Stetson sat atop a sheepskin coat on the empty seat to his left.

He rested one long, muscular leg on the knee of the other and appeared as complacent as a tomcat sunning himself.

She decided there was nothing about this cowboy that seemed cause for concern. And yet…she couldn't remember what he was doing here any more than she could remember what she was doing here.

What was wrong with her anyway? She still felt a little…drunk. But she didn't remember drinking even one full glass of wine at dinner. Strange. She didn't remember much of anything since dinner, she thought as she glanced out the window.

It was dark outside. She frowned as she looked down at her watch. Seven-thirty. Thanksgiving Day. Startled, she realized her last clear memory was driving back from taking Natalie into San Antonio. That had been just a little after five o'clock. How could she have lost two and a half hours? And more importantly, what had happened between then and now?

In that time, she could have flown hundreds— even thousands—of miles from home. But why had she? Worse yet, she still hadn't been able to place the man with her. Of course she had to know him. She'd never get into a plane with a total stranger. Maybe he was a friend of Natalie's.

She looked over at him again, a sense of something at the edge of her memory, something… foreboding.

"You'll have to forgive me, but I'm afraid I don't know who you are or where we're going," she said politely, always a senator's daughter. "I think I might have imbibed a bit too much.'' That wouldn't have been like her at all, but how else could she explain this?

"Don't worry about that now," he said, giving her a smile. "You should get changed before we land." He handed her a large, bulging shopping bag. "I need to speak to the pilot. Since you're still a little woozy, you might want to change right here." With that, he got up and left.

She stared after him. Still a little woozy? But why was that? And why did she need to change?

Inside the bag, she found jeans, a plaid flannel shirt, a winter coat, boots, hat, wool socks and gloves. Wherever they were headed must be cold.

The moment she tried to get to her feet to change, she realized he was right: she *was* woozy. She sat down again and dressed as quickly as she could, considering her body still wasn't reacting sensibly and she had no idea when the man would return. For some reason, the thought of adding more clothing made her somehow feel…safer. Safer from what?

She was trying to puzzle out these odd thoughts, when the plane began its descent. Out the window she could see no lights, no illuminated landmarks, just a nothingness as if she were being dropped into outer space. Waking in a private jet had come with a certain sense of security. Even the stranger hadn't posed any threat. So how did she explain her growing anxiety? It was those dark, frightening images banked at the back of her brain. Were they memories? Or just bad dreams?

She wished he'd return so she could ask him some questions now that she felt a little better. Before they

touched down, she'd like to know what she was doing here. And with him.

The wheels hit and bounced, then settled into the
runway. She'd expected to see more than a narrow
strip of runway lights. They had to be in the middle
of nowhere.

She swallowed hard. What in the— She caught
sight of a hangar as the plane taxied toward it. Behind the hangar, the lights of some town glowed.
She let out the breath she didn't even realize she'd
been holding. She never thought the mere sight of
lights would excite her.

Lights. A memory skidded past. Her heart took
off again as she tried to corner a clear image. She
almost had it, but then the plane stopped and the
cowboy came out of the cockpit.

She looked up at him, frustrated at his timing and,
at the same time, glad to see him. She wanted desperately to extinguish the fear rising in her. This
man had done nothing to make her fearful so why—

Her eyes locked with his. Eyes as black as the
bottom of a well. She felt a start. There *was* something there. But something that justified her fears?

Outside the plane, someone pulled down the
steps. She stood and started toward the door, not
sure she could trust her mind, let alone her instincts.
She'd wanted answers, but right now she just
wanted off this plane and away from this cowboy
and the images flickering in her head. Horrible images that if true—

He stepped in front of her, one large hand absently rubbing the palm of the other as he stared at
her. His look sent a shudder through her.

She dropped her gaze, letting it fall to his large
hands again and felt that flicker of a memory just

beyond her grasp. He quit rubbing his palm and she saw something that stopped her heart dead. Teeth marks.

SETH HAD COME OUT of the cockpit already distracted because of the change in plans. He wouldn't be dropping her at the airstrip after all, but taking her on by helicopter to the cabin. He swore under his breath; he hated changes. But mostly he just wanted this to be over.

Then he'd looked up and seen her.

Even if she hadn't reminded him of Shanna, he'd have been thrown off guard by her. She looked damn good in jeans and a flannel shirt, round and full in all the right places, just as he'd known she would. She'd pulled her wild mane of hair back with a thin lavender ribbon from her dress and rolled up the sleeves on the shirt, exposing lightly freckled, sun-browned forearms.

But it was her face, with those incredible violet eyes, that made him unable to keep his gaze—and his thoughts—off her, no matter how hard he tried to keep his distance.

That's why it took him a moment to realize that more than her clothes had changed.

Although trying hard not to show it, she'd remembered something. It showed in that incredible face, just like every emotion she'd felt so far.

He could only guess what she'd remembered. Not that it mattered now. But as he followed her gaze to the palm of his right hand, at least he knew what had triggered it.

Suddenly the door to the plane yawned open, a gaping dark hole beside him. A gust of cold air whooshed in, scented with pine and snow. God, it had been so long. The air brought with it a rush of remembrances, some so painful he felt as if he'd been blindsided.

Of course she took that opportunity to dart for the open doorway. He dropped a hand to her shoulder and gently pulled her back.

Her eyes widened as she lifted her face to him. "Who are you?" Her voice had an edge to it, as if warning him that he just might not know whom he was dealing with.

"It doesn't matter who I am," he said. "It isn't about me."

"Then who is it about?" she asked. "My father?"

"I don't know. Neither will you until we get to the cabin."

"The cabin?" Her gaze refused to release him. It was as if she could see into his very soul. From the disgust on her face, she didn't like what she saw there. "You're not telling me anything."

"It's the best I can do." Seth could see that wasn't good enough. "It will all be clear when we get to the cabin." Indecision played across her features. "I hope it won't be necessary for me to drug you again," he said softly.

The violet eyes widened for an instant, then narrowed in an emotion he recognized only too clearly. Fury.

"Good," he said. "It appears we understand each other."

OH, SHE UNDERSTOOD him all right. She'd been kidnapped! The frightening images in her head had been real! Memories scudded by like dark ominous clouds. The sound of him behind her, the overwhelming arms tightening around her, the hand covering her mouth. Screaming inside. Fighting. Fighting fruitlessly in helpless terror. Then the prick of a needle in her arm. Then nothing.

The bastard had drugged her! And now he'd threatened to do it again unless she cooperated. She glared at him. Tears stung her eyes but she would not cry. Tears would show weakness. She had to be strong, keep her head, use her head.

He pulled on his sheepskin coat, settled the Stetson on his head, his gaze steady, impassive and honed in on her like radar, but calm. Too calm. A shiver raced through her. A man who'd just kidnapped Texas Senator James Marshall McCord's daughter should be worried as all get-out. Only a crazy man wouldn't be. A crazy man. Or a man who had nothing to lose. She stared at him, afraid he just might be both.

"Let's go," he said as he picked up her clothes and stuffed them into a backpack from behind his seat. He nudged her forward, his hand firmly on her shoulder. "Watch your step."

She didn't miss the warning in his words. But she had no intention of doing anything that would give him an excuse to drug her again. Drugged, she didn't stand a chance.

At the open doorway she stopped to look out. Snow. It shone, silver-white against the dark of night; it covered the ground as far as she could see. Whoever had opened the door didn't seem to be around anymore, but nearby a helicopter waited.

The cowboy took hold of her the moment they stepped onto the frozen ground and drew her toward the chopper, his hand clamped firmly around her upper arm, his body pressed against her side.

She looked around, hoping there would be other people, someone she could call to for help. But the airstrip was empty and a large white expanse of open field ran for a good mile in the direction of the lights of the town. The only building, the hangar, sat dark and empty.

As she neared the whirring blades of the helicopter, wind spun the fallen snow, showering her in white ice-cold powder. The door opened and she was pushed up into a seat behind the pilot. Her kidnapper slid in next to her, his thigh against hers in the tight confines of the chopper.

Before she could buckle up, the helicopter lifted off, spinning away into the night. She pressed herself to the side window, pulling away from him. All she could see below was the shine of the snow broken occasionally by the dark fringe of the evergreens and the rise and fall of mountains as the chopper skimmed low over them.

Without a word, he reached across to snap her seat belt closed, forcing her to touch him again.

His closeness assaulted her senses. But this time, his male scent evoked memories of the kidnapping, the same way his muscled thigh against her leg reminded her how easily he could overpower her. The images danced before her. Pouring rain. Darkness. His arms clamped around her and the helplessness she'd felt as he'd dragged her away from her car, away from her life.

She looked back. The lights of the town were gone. Slowly she turned to stare ahead again into the darkness, her heartbeat a deafening roar in her ears. Tears blurred her eyes as sobs rose in her throat, choking her. *She'd been kidnapped.* The ramifications had finally hit home. All her bravado, all her control, all her toughness deserted her. She was afraid, ice-in-the-veins afraid.

THEY WEREN'T IN THE AIR but a few minutes when the helicopter dropped low, hovered for a moment, then set down in a cloud of whirling snow.

"Ladies first," her cowboy kidnapper said as he leaned over to open her door.

She glanced at the pilot, but immediately changed her mind about making a desperate attempt to gain his help. The man had to be in on this.

She reached down, her fingers fumbling with the seat belt buckle. Suddenly the cowboy's hands covered hers and she felt the buckle release. No more stalling. This was it.

She slid out of the seat and down, torn between the fears that he planned to leave her out here alone and that he was coming with her. He stepped down beside her, grasping her arm again as he leaned over her, shielding her from the pounding ice crystals as the chopper lifted off.

Within moments the whir of its blades died away, as did the lights of the helicopter. She waited for the darkness to close in. But it didn't. An almost full moon rose above the low-hanging clouds, illuminating them and casting an eerie light across the snow. In that strange light, she could see that they'd landed in a small, isolated meadow. Past it, she could see nothing but snow, pine trees and mountains. No sign of life. Except for the man beside her.

Her pulse drummed in her ears as she looked over at him, and she felt her first real sense of hysteria since she'd been abducted. She hadn't been alone with this man in the jet. Or the helicopter. But now, in this isolated part of some backwoods, she was completely alone with her kidnapper. It hit her with such force, her knees threatened to give way beneath her. What did he plan to do with her now?

Next to her, he stood, his head cocked as if listening. Then his attention swung to her. "Come on." He took her hand and she trudged in his wake, wading through the fallen snow, trying to keep up and, at the same time, see where she was going. The country looked wild and unsettled. She hated to imagine where he might be taking her.

Then he topped a small rise and she saw the cabin. It loomed up out of the darkness, a small A-frame, as picturesque as a ski lodge in the Swiss Alps.

He'd told her she'd find out everything at the cabin, but no lights shone from the windows, no smoke curled up from the chimney, nor did any tracks mar the snow. It didn't look as if anyone were home. Had he lied to her just to get her up here without a fight? She doubted that as she followed him across the meadow. He'd also threatened to drug her again. She didn't doubt he would have gotten her here one way or the other.

By the time Levi reached the front steps of the cabin, she just hoped it was warm and dry inside. She didn't think past that, afraid to.

She followed the cowboy up the untracked snowy steps to the front deck. He seemed to hesitate at the door. She followed his gaze to a ramp off one end of the deck. It too was covered in fresh, unblemished snow.

She watched him frown as he looked back at the steps, as if he'd also noticed the lack of tracks and was bothered by it. Then he tried the door. It opened in his hand. She saw him reach inside and an instant later, a light came on. He quickly stepped in and pulled her in behind him.

The cabin was old-fashioned, quaint, although definitely male. She wondered if it was his, and hoped it was because the place made her believe that the man who lived here wasn't dangerous.

He left her standing in the middle of the room. Not that he ever really let her out of his sight as he opened the doors to each of the rooms, seeming to look for something. Or someone.

The clock on the wall said it was only eight forty-five and yet she felt exhausted. Had it been less than five hours since her father had made a toast at their Thanksgiving dinner on the ranch?

She realized her kidnapper had stopped searching the rooms. He stood looking at her, frowning, his gaze obviously troubled.

"What is it?" she asked, her fear rising.

He shook his head, turned and began rummaging through drawers, pulling out items, which he thrust into his backpack. That relaxed Texas cowboy on the jet was gone; this man was anxious and on alert. She watched in alarm as he threw things into the backpack, including a pistol, then ushered her out the front door again, closing it behind them.

He stopped on the deck, appearing to listen again, then without warning, swung her up into his arms and took one long-legged step to the corner of the small deck. He lowered her to the ground below.

What in the world?

"Don't move," he ordered in a whisper before he jumped down beside her. She watched him break off a limb from a nearby pine tree, urging her to walk across the open space beyond the A-frame toward the darkness. Behind them, he began to brush the fresh snow over their tracks.

Levi stared ahead into the wall of dark pines, cold and sick inside. Where was he taking her now?

Once in the dense trees, he took the lead again, drawing her deeper into their seclusion as the land rose sharply. She climbed until she thought her lungs would burst from the high altitude and cold.

By the time another structure appeared, the cold and the climb had zapped her energy. She was tired and ready to quit walking. He didn't even seem to be breathing hard, although he'd been the one bucking the deep, soft snow, making somewhat of a trail for her.

The dark edge of a log structure materialized out of the night and the pines. Slowly it took shape. Rustic. Small. Isolated. Barely a shack. More like a four-sided lean-to. Nothing like the A-frame they'd left behind.

She didn't realize she'd stopped walking until she felt the tug on her arm.

"Hey," he said, and stepped so close to her that he forced out the night air. She stared down at his gloved hand on hers. "It's not the Hilton, but it'll be warmer and drier than out here."

She didn't answer. Couldn't. Her throat felt swollen with the tears she'd held at bay. All she could think about was what he planned to do to her in there. It was the kind of place that might already have bodies buried under the worn floorboards—if it had a floor at all.

Her kidnapper lifted her chin until she was looking directly up under the brim of the Stetson and straight into his shadowed face. She couldn't see his eyes but she could feel his heated gaze.

"Look, I know you're cold and tired," he said, as if she were simply rebelling against the accommodations. He must have felt her trembling. "You can warm up here and rest."

It was the most he'd said to her in hours. But it was the tone that made her want to cry. Why was he being so nice now?

From inside the backpack, he took out a large flashlight, but he didn't turn it on.

Levi glanced in the direction they'd come. She could see the lights the cowboy had left on in the cabin below them. They cast a gentle glow across the snow, making the winter scene warm and inviting. Why had he made her walk all the way up this mountainside?

He opened the shack door, seemed to listen for a moment, then motioned for her to follow. It wasn't until they were inside that he turned on the flashlight.

Her heart sank as she saw that the one room was pretty much as she'd feared it would be: empty, except for years of dust, an old table, a couple of mismatched chairs and a cot.

His look brought the fear back in a heartbeat. "You can lie down over there," he said, motioning to the cot. He reached into the backpack for a wool blanket and tossed it to her.

She swallowed hard. "What do you want with me?" Her voice broke and she hated the vulnerability she heard in it.

He stepped to her, letting the beam of the flashlight bore into the dusty worn wood at their feet as he gazed down at her. When he spoke his voice was soft, almost compassionate, but behind the words was an urgency, a warning. "I just want you to sit

quietly until I tell you otherwise. Do you understand?''

She nodded and stepped past him to the cot, her
heart aching for her family, for home. How long
would she have to stay in this cabin with this man?
Or would he ever let her leave here?

The flashlight went out, plunging them into a
chilly, thick darkness. She waited for her eyes to
adjust, telling herself this might be her chance.
Maybe, if she could use one of the cot legs as a
weapon...

She heard him prying boards from the window.
A little of the snowy night spilled in. She could see
him now, sitting in the chair he'd pulled up in front
of the glassless opening. She reached down, feeling
around with her hand. If she could get one of the
legs free—

''Don't,'' he said.

Her gaze shot up. He wasn't facing her, but intent
on looking through the window opening with what
appeared to be some kind of binoculars. Night-
vision goggles?

''Don't be foolish,'' he continued conversationally, still not looking in her direction. ''You
wouldn't stand a chance against me.'' His voice was
low and soft and unthreatening, but the words hit
her like stones. ''Before you can get up and cross
the room, I'll stop you. Because I won't have a lot
of time to deal with you, it might be painful. So I
suggest you just do as I ask. Hopefully, we won't
be here long.''

She straightened slowly, holding her breath, afraid
to make a sound or move too quickly. Who was this
man and what did he want with her? Levi stared at
him, sure he was watching the A-frame where the

helicopter had dropped them off. Waiting. For what? A ransom drop?

She heard him shift in the chair. She prayed that money was all he wanted. Her father would pay the ransom, even a very large one. Then she would go home.

Otherwise…she could only bide her time. Wait for him to make a mistake. Even men like him had to make mistakes. And she'd be ready when he did.

THROUGH THE GLASSES, Seth watched the A-frame and the snowy landscape around it. He could see the twin tracks where the helicopter had set down in the snow and the two pairs of boot prints that led up to the front steps of the cabin.

He waited and watched, trying to nail down exactly what was bothering him. The change of plans. He was supposed to have met Wally at the airstrip. He was supposed to have handed over the woman. Job done.

But when he'd gone up to see the pilot, he'd been informed that a helicopter would be waiting to take them to the cabin. He'd told himself he was just being overly suspicious. Or maybe his apprehension just had to do with the woman. That she'd reminded him of Shanna filled him with a sense of dread he couldn't shake off. Returning to Montana after all these years, facing all the memories and regrets, well, that was also taking its toll.

He squeezed his eyes for a moment to chase away the thoughts. Thoughts of Shanna. Thoughts of this woman. Both were all tangled into a knot of heartache.

Damn. He'd wanted to be back in Texas, this woman no longer his concern. Instead he was in a cold miner's shack on a snowy mountainside fighting a terrible sense of déjà vu, as if history were about to repeat itself and, like last time, there wasn't a damned thing he could do about it.

Had the woman thrown off his instincts so much that he was jumping at shadows? Seth shook his head in disgust. He was going to look like a damn fool when he had to tromp down this mountain to deliver the woman.

Behind him, she was no longer moving around. He could hear her breathing softly. Had she finally given up and fallen asleep? Or was she sitting, waiting anxiously, wondering what to expect now? *Welcome to the club.*

He tried to relax. Everything had gone fine—at least at his end. Better than fine. He had her and all he had to do was hand her over to Wally. So where was Wally? Why had he changed the plan? It was so unlike him.

Seth scanned the landscape around the A-frame, seeing nothing but trees and snow. Fool. He should be in that cabin right now with a fire roaring, a mug of hot coffee and—

The A-frame exploded right before his eyes. The flash blinded him as the cabin turned into a fireball. A few seconds later, the blast echoed in his ears. He stared, dumbfounded, struck by that sense of déjà vu. And doom.

First, the change of plans. Now, this. He stared at the burning cabin, then turned to the woman on the cot, and a jolt of something stronger and much more potent than adrenaline raced through him. Cold, hard fear. Who the hell *was* this woman?

Chapter Three

"Who are you?"

Levi awoke with a start, amazed she'd actually fallen asleep. Probably the side effects of that drug he'd given her earlier. The sound of an explosion rang in her ears, but only the smell of smoke made her believe she hadn't dreamed it.

Before she could move, she looked up to find the cowboy standing over her, yelling down at her, his words making no sense. What had blown up?

"Who are you?" he asked again.

She sat up, pulled the scratchy wool blanket to her and gazed up at him, afraid. "What?" was all she got out before he jerked her to her feet.

"*Who the hell are you?*" he demanded as he ripped off the blanket and threw it onto the cot.

"You know who I am," she cried, staring at him as if he were a madman as well as a kidnapper.

"Tell me your *name*," he demanded from between clenched teeth.

"Levi."

He frowned. "Levi? Levi who?"

She couldn't understand what it was he wanted

from her or why he was so upset. "McCord. Levi McCord."

He released her as if she were a live wire. "*McCord?* Levi McCord? Not—" He stared at her. "Tell me you're not related to *Senator* McCord."

Was this some sort of trick? "He's my father."

He swore loudly, raked a hand through his hair, then looked at her again as if he'd never seen her before. "*You're* James Marshall McCord's daughter?"

"Olivia McCord," she said almost indignantly. "Levi's a nickname." She frowned as a thought buzzed past like a bullet. "But you had to know that when you kidnapped me. Why else—" She stopped, even more confused.

He let out a harsh laugh and looked up at the ceiling, still shaking his head. He *was* a madman. Or he really *hadn't* known who she was. Or both. He swung his gaze back to her and cursed, his eyes dark and disturbed.

She came fully awake with an anger of her own. "Who are *you?*" she demanded. Her head had cleared some from the short, fitful, exhausted sleep and the rude awakening and the drug he'd given her earlier. "You kidnapped me and you didn't even know who I was?" What kind of sense did that make? She was even more angry than she had been. The anger felt so much better than the fear. "Talk to me, damn you."

"Not now," he growled as he thrust the flashlight into the backpack and pulled the drawstring closed, his movements hurried, anxious. "We have to get out of here."

He stepped to the door, opened it and stood silhouetted against the snowfall, waiting impatiently for her.

She moved as if sleepwalking to the window opening in the wall and looked out. Below her in the clearing, what was left of the A-frame burned bright in the night. Her heart thudded at the ramifications. They could have been in that cabin!

"Come on," he ordered when she didn't move toward him. "Trust me, now isn't the time to give me trouble."

She turned to look at him, feeling the effects of adrenaline and exhaustion, anger and fear. She didn't move, just stared at him, determined not to take another step until she had an explanation. "Tell me. Now."

He shook his head in obvious frustration. "Let me put it to you simply. Somebody firebombed the cabin because they thought we were inside it. I don't know how close they are or if they've already found our tracks and are headed up this mountain right now, but I think they're probably not going to give up until they kill us. How's that?"

She swallowed hard. "Why would someone want to kill us?"

"You tell me."

He was blaming *her* for this?

"But I'm not staying here to find out," he said before she could respond. "Now get your butt out that door or I'll drag you. Believe me, you won't slow me down that much. At least not for long."

She didn't like the sound of that. The moment she moved toward him, he grabbed her and propelled her through the open doorway. It was still dark outside, except for the fiery glow where the A-frame had been.

The air felt colder. Or maybe it was just the cold inside her as he pulled her through the pines, his grip strong and firm and unrelenting. She had to run to keep up with his long stride. They dropped down the other side of the mountain, away from the smell of charred wood.

She felt dazed. Who had blown up the A-frame? Why had the man now dragging her off this mountain kidnapped her without even knowing who she was? It made no sense. Nothing made any sense. But if he meant her real harm, wouldn't he have just killed her and left her behind at the shack? Or...was she worth more to him alive?

The air suddenly turned white and wet with fog. He kept moving. The mist wove through the snow-laden pines, growing denser and denser until she couldn't see but a few feet in front of her. He slowed a little, not much.

Then she heard it. The sound of water lapping softly. Moments later, they stumbled on the bank of what appeared to be a wide creek. On the snowy edge, he finally stopped and she leaned over, her hands on her knees, to catch her breath.

Without warning, he picked her up and tossed her over his shoulder like a sack of potatoes, reminding her again how strong he was as he waded into the icy water.

She started to protest, but he stopped her with a low warning growl. Common sense told her this was not the time.

He headed upstream into the fog, his hand resting on her rump as she bounced along on his shoulder.

She thought she heard a helicopter. He must have, too, because he stopped for a moment to listen, then continued upstream.

Finally he put her down on the opposite bank and climbed out beside her. She watched him through a film of fog as he went to a spot along the bank and pulled branches back from a canoe.

The movement came out of the smudged darkness of the pines off to her right. She saw it from the corner of her eye, but didn't get a sound out before the movement became a man. He seemed a part of the fog, a blur of white clothing and mask, until she saw a rifle in his gloved hands. She didn't have time to think, let alone react. Unlike her kidnapper. He turned, sensing danger. Just as the attacker swung the rifle butt at her, the cowboy grabbed for the barrel and jerked, throwing the attacker off balance.

The blow did little more than send her sprawling into the snow. But by then the cowboy had sent the attacker flying. The man landed on his back hard, the rifle falling from his hands and sliding down the bank into the cold stream. As the cowboy leaped after him, she saw the attacker pull something from his boot. A knife blade glittered as the two struggled in the snow.

She froze as she watched them fight, her thoughts frantic. What should she do? Run! But run where? She got to her feet but couldn't see more than a few feet in the dense fog and didn't know the terrain, didn't even know where she was. Think! The canoe. Take the canoe. She rushed over to it and was hurriedly trying to pull it out of its hiding place when she heard a splash behind her and swung around.

"Did he hurt you?" her kidnapper asked, sounding almost concerned for her. He picked up his Stetson from the snow and shoved it down on his head, then stumbled toward her, his breathing labored. He was covered in snow, and blood seeped from a wound on his temple.

"Are you hurt?" he demanded. He wiped at the wound. It didn't look deep or life threatening.

She shook her head and looked past him. The attacker was gone. "Where is he?" she asked, her voice breaking.

The cowboy pointed across the creek. "He got away."

She stared into the darkness of the pines. "What makes you so sure he won't be back?"

"I'm not, but I would imagine he'll go for help. He was wounded. Not bad. Just a cut on his arm, but enough that I don't think he'll be back—at least for a while. By then we'll be gone."

From behind a wall of tears, she saw him reach for her, but he didn't seem to have enough fight left in him to stop her as she sidestepped him. He let his hand drop as she moved to the edge of the water where the two had been fighting. She dropped to her knees in the churned snow, wishing for some way to confirm the cowboy's story—or her worst fears. Had the other man come to rescue her…or kill her?

"From here on out, you're going to have to trust me," her kidnapper said behind her, his voice rough. "Or at least do as I tell you."

"How do I know you didn't have the cabin booby-trapped so it would blow up when someone came after me?" Levi snapped. She was angry and afraid, but equally tired and cold. "Obviously you knew someone was going to come. Isn't that why you dragged me up the mountain to that shack where you could watch for them? Isn't that why you hid this canoe by the creek?"

"It isn't a creek. It's a river," he said as he came up behind her. "And I didn't hide the canoe. Its owner did, years ago."

She stepped back away from him. The cowboy had just made his first mistake.

"Don't come any closer," she warned, aiming the pistol she'd found in the snow.

He stopped and raised his hands, palms out. "I take it you've fired one of those before?"

"Many times."

He nodded as if he should have known, the way his day was going.

"I want some answers and I want them now," Levi said.

"You definitely pick your moments," he said with a tired sigh.

"Who was that?" she demanded.

The cowboy shook his head. "I have no idea."

"Why was he trying to kill you?"

"I would assume he thought it would be easier to knock you unconscious, kill me first, then you," he answered matter-of-factly. "But that's just a guess."

She groaned. "How do you know he didn't intend to push me out of the way, to save me from you?"

"With the butt of his rifle?"

"Maybe that's the best he could do at short notice," she argued.

"Maybe."

She waited for him to convince her she was wrong. He didn't even try. "Give me one good reason why I shouldn't shoot you?"

He pushed his Stetson back from his forehead. "Because there's probably more of them out there and if you fire that pistol, the sound will only give them our location." He said it softly, conversationally and with an arrogance that made her trigger finger itch. "Plus, you're smart enough to think that I just might be the lesser of two evils."

"You're the one who *kidnapped* me. Why would I think you're less dangerous?"

"Then shoot me." He started toward her. "Because, otherwise, we've got to get out of here."

"You come any closer and I'll—" She gripped the pistol in her hand, feeling the cold steel of the trigger just beneath her finger. He stepped up to her. "Don't—"

With ease and speed, he snatched the gun from her hand and stuffed it into the waistband of his jeans. "Don't ever pull a gun on me again unless you intend to use it."

She stood trembling as he turned his back on her. He pushed the canoe into the water and held it steady before he settled his gaze on her again. "Get in."

The order made her bristle. Around them the fog seemed to be getting colder, wetter and more dense by the minute. "I should have shot you when I had the chance," she said, glaring at him.

"Probably," he agreed. "But since you didn't, get into the canoe." He swore when she didn't move. "My name's Seth. And I didn't kidnap you, not exactly. Now get in before you get us both killed."

She glanced across the river, then moved to the

canoe and got in without a word as he pushed them off.

The current caught the small craft, sucking it into the fog bank. She wrapped her arms around herself, huddling in the front of the boat. There were so many questions she wanted to ask Seth—if that was his real name—but she knew he wasn't going to tell her anything until he was good and ready. And she couldn't be sure he wasn't right, that there weren't others out there, just waiting to attack them. So she remained silent, something extremely hard for her to do under even ordinary circumstances. Only nothing was ordinary about this. Or the man she was with.

She felt him paddle them out into the fast water, as if he'd done it a hundred times. Maybe he had. She had the feeling this man could do anything. Who was he anyway? And what was she doing with him, as if she had a choice? She shivered, remembering the look he'd given her when he'd taken the gun from her hand. Instinctively she knew he was dangerous. So why had he saved her life? Not once, but twice. Or had he?

She stared into the fog, her brain and body numb. Part of her feared an attack from the banked whiteness. Another part feared she was in more danger from the man in the canoe than anyone who came out of the fog.

The river lapped at the sides of the boat; the fog rushed by. Where were they headed now? She felt caught up in something bigger than herself as the canoe swept down the river with nothing to gauge distance by other than the feel of the wind on her face and the whisper of the fog as it sailed past.

Time seemed suspended. She watched Seth paddle and felt like the water, racing toward something. But what?

Then in the distance she heard the sound of a waterfall.

Chapter Four

Senator James Marshall McCord's daughter! Seth still couldn't believe it. As he paddled down the river in the cloud-veiled moonlight and fog, he tried to convince himself that it was some kind of terrible mistake. A case of mistaken identity. A glitch in paperwork. He couldn't have snatched the wrong woman. His instructions had been too specific.

Exactly. His instructions had been too specific. There *was* no mistake. He was supposed to abduct the senator's daughter. The question was why?

Only one person could answer that: Wally.

In Seth's business, jumping to conclusions was dangerous. So he fought hard not to as the canoe drifted through the fog, the water lapping softly at the side, the air cold and wet with the promise of more snow.

Because right now the conclusion was that he'd been set up. Not just for the kidnapping but for the woman's murder. And that dishonor was to have been awarded posthumously.

The problem was, he couldn't believe anyone would go to this kind of trouble to frame him, let alone kill him. He just wasn't worth it.

But Olivia McCord was, he reminded himself.

And, somehow, he had to keep her safe until he could get her back to her family and straighten this out.

So far he'd been going on gut instinct. He'd known something was wrong at the airstrip, when Wally hadn't met them and instead had them choppered in to the cabin. At Wally's cabin, everything had just felt...wrong.

Once the cabin had blown to smithereens—well, his instincts told him that straightening this out wasn't going to be easy.

Olivia McCord. He studied her dark huddled form at the other end of the canoe as he let the craft drift, the fog rushing around it, the banks blurring by, white with snow, the water deep and dark and cold. The name didn't suit her. Olivia was too soft a name, too womanly, too feminine sounding. That woman, the one he'd glimpsed in the glare of the car headlights, reminded him too much of Shanna.

But "Levi" fit the spitfire who'd drawn down on him with the loaded pistol. He shook his head, the difference between Shanna and this woman never more clear.

He remembered the day he'd tried to get Shanna to learn to shoot so she could defend herself. She'd finally handed the pistol back to him, more afraid of the gun than anyone who might want to harm her.

Seth blinked. No, Levi was nothing like Shanna when she had a .44 Magnum in her hand. But there was that other side of her. The soft, sexy, definitely female woman in the lavender dress. The one that reminded him of Shanna. The one he had to avoid at all costs.

He swore under his breath. It didn't matter who Levi reminded him of, what he called her or how he cared to think of her, she was still the Texas senator's daughter. And Seth Gantry was in a world of hurt.

"Excuse me."

He blinked at the sound of her voice and realized she was staring at him, the same way he'd been staring at her.

"Sounds like a waterfall," she pointed out.

He nodded. The roar of rushing water grew louder as the canoe floated through the fog toward it.

"We aren't going over it, right?" She sounded more annoyed than worried, as if going over a waterfall would be the last straw.

"Don't worry," he said, thinking they had a lot more to worry about than simply drowning. "We'll be getting out pretty soon."

"Where exactly are we?" She sounded weary, as if some of the fight had gone out of her. He only wished. He had enough to fight without adding her to the list.

"On the Boulder River. In Montana." He figured he owed her that much.

"Montana?" She made it sound as though he'd taken her to the North Pole. But even Montana was a long way from home for a Texas girl.

"About twenty miles south of Big Timber." The canoe rounded the bend in the river, the waterfall a thunder ahead of them. He could feel the icy spray of the falls in the air and see it freezing on the rocks along the high bank, frosty-white.

He reached out to grab an eddy with his paddle

and the canoe swung into a large washed-out cave in the rocks.

Levi didn't take any urging; she was out the moment the canoe touched solid ground again. Did she think she was safe now?

"You're from here, aren't you."

It wasn't a question. Actually, it sounded more like an accusation. And she had to yell it to be heard over the thundering water.

He climbed out beside her, then let the canoe go. He watched until it disappeared into the fog, into the roar of the waterfall. "Yeah, I grew up around here."

She nodded, studying him with eyes that saw too much. "They'll know we didn't go over with the canoe," she said. She was close enough she didn't have to yell; too close for comfort. "Now what?"

"Now we steal a vehicle."

She raised a brow. "Just like that."

He hoped. Steal a vehicle. Get to a phone. Call Wally. That's as far as he'd thought it out. But he didn't want to have to explain his lack of a real plan to this woman, so with an urgency that had nothing to do with whoever might be after them, he led the way out of the rocks, motioning for her to keep quiet. He stayed in the shelter of the pines, sneaking along through the trees and rocks.

The fog thinned as they left the river bottom, but the low-hanging clouds made the air smell wet. It hadn't started to snow yet, but Seth knew it would. Soon.

At one point, he thought he heard a helicopter again, but he never saw its lights.

The old farmhouse sat back against a wall of tan

bluffs and large pines. The house itself was probably still used in the spring, when huge flocks of sheep were herded up into the Absaroka and Beartooth wilderness to graze for the summer. But right now it sat closed up and empty.

Off to its right, a large once-red barn loomed out of the clouds, a black wide hole in the front where the double doors hung open. In the pitch blackness, something glittered dully. A bumper.

The bumper belonged to an ancient faded green International Harvester pickup. From the look of the cow manure and yellowed grass stuck to the tire wells, the truck had been used maybe as recently as early fall.

He watched Levi eye the pickup skeptically and him even more. He tried not to let it hurt his feelings as he popped the hood, hoping the rancher hadn't taken out the battery for the winter. While looking a little corroded, the battery sat snugly in its corner, held in place with wire. He touched an end of wire between the two terminals and got a spark. They were in business.

Feeling lucky, he slammed the hood and swung around to the passenger side of the pickup to let Levi in. The door groaned as he dragged it open and offered her a seat. She looked cold. He hoped the heater worked.

Going around to the driver's side, he shrugged out of the backpack, tossed it onto the seat and reached around the steering column, hoping to find the keys in the ignition. His luck wasn't *that* good.

He could feel her dubious look as he lay down on his back on the floorboard under the steering column, the door open and his legs hanging out. He was glad for once that he'd picked up a few useful talents in his wayward youth.

As the engine rumbled to life, he shot Levi a glance, hoping to see grudging admiration in her face. Or at least a little respect.

Instead she gave him a look that said *If you're so smart, then why are people trying to kill you?* Or maybe he was just thinking that himself.

He slid out of the truck, grousing at what a hard woman she was to impress, but before he could turn to get back in, he felt a boot connect hard with his butt. The unexpected momentum sent him sprawling headfirst onto the barn floor.

Behind him he heard the driver's side door slam, the motor rev and the clutch pop. As the old truck roared backward out of the barn, he leaped to his feet and ran after it. Blamed woman!

She was frantically searching for first gear when he reached her side of the pickup. Just as he grabbed for the door handle, she slammed down the lock with her elbow. Damn her! She found first gear, popped the clutch again, but her inexperience driving on snow gave him a few seconds. He flung himself over the hood to the passenger side and jumped on the running board as the less-than-great rubber on the tires spun for a moment, then caught. He tried the door, not surprised to find it locked as well.

Clinging to the moving vehicle by the side mirror, he tapped on the glass. Levi glanced over at him. He mouthed the word *stop.* But she turned back to her driving, getting the pickup rolling along at a pretty good clip as she headed for the main road.

He held onto the mirror, quickly assessing the situation as he saw in the pickup's headlights the row of low-limbed pine trees coming up on his side of the narrow road. He slammed an elbow against the side window. The window shuddered but didn't break. He heard a shriek from inside the truck but she made no attempt to slow down. Big surprise.

Just as he'd figured, she drove close enough to the pines lining the driveway that the branches whipped him and did their best to knock him off the running board. This woman was starting to get to him.

Just past the last pine tree, she threw on the brakes. The change in momentum swung him around the mirror and smacked his hip into the fender, but he managed to get his feet back on the running board before she got the truck going again. She was getting better at driving on snow.

Tired of fooling with her, he elbowed the side window once more. This time the glass shattered, showering into the cab, bringing a satisfying oath from inside.

Quickly he reached in and pulled the door handle up. The door swung open and he leaped in, slamming it behind him before she had a chance to do anything more than shift gears.

He didn't look at her. "Stop the truck."

Not surprisingly, she didn't jump to his quiet command. In fact, she didn't even respond.

"Stop the truck now or so help me, Levi—"

She hit the brakes, almost putting him through the windshield. She flung open her door and jumped out at a run. He slid across the seat, slipping the truck into neutral to keep it from dying as it rolled to a stop, and went after her. In two long strides, he caught her by the collar of her coat.

"Are you crazy?" he demanded.

"I'm the one who should be asking *you* that," she snapped, anger flashing in her eyes. Her breath came out frosty-white in the night. "I didn't kidnap *you.*"

He let out a sigh. "If you could just let me get us to a phone, I could prove to you that I didn't *kidnap* you."

She mugged a face at him. "Why should I believe anything you tell me? You haven't told me anything."

"Excuse *me*. I've been a little busy trying to keep us alive." She didn't seem in the least appreciative and he wondered what it would take. "I told you my name."

"Seth? Seth what?"

"Gantry."

She raised a brow. "If Seth Gantry is even your name."

"It is," he replied indignantly.

They stood glaring at each other, breathing hard, eyeing each other with distrust. He could see doubt in her expression; she didn't believe they were still in danger. Maybe she didn't want to believe she'd ever been in danger—other than from him.

He tried to think of something he could say to gain her trust but gave up. He had to face it: she wasn't going to go along with him anymore. At least not willingly. And he was in no mood to fight her.

"I hate to have to do this," he said. Pulling the handcuffs from his coat pocket with one hand, he let go of her collar and grasped her right wrist.

She tried to struggle out of his hold. "You

wouldn't," she said, giving him a haughty look when all else had failed.

"You'd be surprised what I'd do right now," he muttered. He snapped one of the loops closed on her wrist. "You're lucky I don't take you over my knee." He hauled her around to the passenger side. "Get in the truck." She had the good sense not to cross him again. The moment she climbed in, he fastened the other loop to the seat frame.

From behind the pickup seat, he dug out a threadbare farm jacket and a chunk of old cardboard. He stuffed it into the broken side window as best he could, closed the door and went around to the driver's side and slid in, only to find her searching through his backpack with her free left hand.

"The pistol isn't in there," he said. He closed the door and snatched the backpack from her before she decided to use the flashlight on him.

Once on the main road, a blacktopped two-lane, he headed north toward Big Timber, glad the low clouds and the darkness provided protective cover from any aircraft. Then the snow began to fall, large white flakes drifting lazily down, and he knew they stood a good chance of not being seen from the air. That still left the possibility of a roadblock though.

But he didn't think that was likely since he didn't believe the people after them were FBI or any other law enforcement group. Yet.

He felt better. But then he always felt better on the move—even when he had no idea where he was headed or what waited around the next bend.

"So what now?" Levi asked. "I assume you have a plan."

He stared at the road. He couldn't believe she

expected him to devise an infallible plan while he was saving their lives, escaping killers and stealing wheels. "No reason to have a plan until you need one."

"You don't have the foggiest idea what you're doing, do you?" she asked incredulously.

He glanced over at her. "I'm flying by the seat of my pants here. I'm sorry if you have a problem with that, princess."

"Don't call me that," she snapped, but all the fight seemed to have gone out of her.

He felt a wave of guilt and searched around for something to say. When words failed him, he got the heater going, pleased to hear it hum and even more happy when a little warm air spit from it. Maybe a bit of heat would help her.

He happened to catch his reflection in the rear-view mirror. No wonder she'd thought he was the crazy one. Between the dried blood on his temple and the dark stubble of a day's growth of beard on his chin and the look in his eyes, he appeared crazed. Hell, he *was* crazed. He always felt that way when someone was trying to kill him.

He turned his attention to the highway. Ahead, the new snow melted the moment it touched the pavement; fog rose like lost spirits in the headlights. Inside the pickup, even with only a coat and cardboard stuffed in the broken window, it was starting to warm up and it felt good.

"Don't you think you ought to at least tell me what I'm doing here?" Levi asked in a no-nonsense tone.

This was a woman used to giving orders. Too bad he wasn't in the habit of taking them.

When he didn't answer immediately, she snapped, "Look, you got me into this. You kidnapped me or whatever you'd like to call it, almost got me killed and you didn't even know who I was. The very least you owe me is an explanation."

Whew. Warm this woman up and she was instantly on the fight again. He shook his head, grinning to himself. He liked that she wasn't down for the count. Through it all, she'd stayed pretty cool. He had to hand it to her, he didn't think he would have been as calm in the same situation. Hell, he didn't feel all that calm right now.

"I don't expect you to believe me. I just did a favor for a friend who asked me to pick you up and bring you to Montana." He shifted into fourth as the pickup began to move downhill at a pretty good clip. Ahead, the highway remained empty of traffic—at least as far as he could see through the snowfall. "So I did."

"You have to be kidding."

On the whole, he thought she'd taken it fairly well.

"It never crossed your mind that picking me up and taking me across state borders to Montana might be a federal offense more commonly known as *kidnapping?*" she demanded.

"I'm familiar with the law."

"Oh, really? Is your friend also familiar with the law?"

"He's the one who taught it to me," Seth said, trying not to lose his temper. "Wally's a private investigator."

Disbelief raised her voice an octave or two. "Without knowing who I was or why you were doing it, you agreed, just like that, without even asking?"

"There really wasn't a lot of time to ask questions. I know a request like that might seem strange to you—" he saw her eyebrow shoot skyward in answer "—but I trust Wally with my life."

"Really? So how do you explain what happened back there at the cabin and the man who tried to kill you at the river?"

"I can't." The pickup rattled down the highway, windshield wipers thunking back and forth to the howl of the heater. "Not yet, anyway."

"That's it?" She'd no doubt been expecting more.

"I'm afraid so, until I talk to Wally. But as soon as I know, you'll be the first to hear about it." He knew that response wasn't going to be enough for her, however. She was good and warmed up and on the fight again.

"Let me guess," she said, giving him an I-know-your-type look. "A lot of money was involved, right?"

He flinched at the insult. "I've been having some financial problems lately and yeah, the money—I needed the money, all right?" He'd had more than his share of bad luck lately and the work couldn't have come along at a better time. Wally had offered him a bonus if he did the job with the utmost discretion. *Discreet* was Seth's middle name. So what was he apologizing for?

"But the money wasn't the reason I took the job," he said, realizing how true that was. If it had been anyone but Wally, Seth would have demanded to know a whole lot more—such as who the woman was and why he was "apprehending" her. But he trusted Wally—and Wally had promised to tell him everything as soon as the jet touched down in Montana.

In retrospect, Seth knew Wally had purposely *not* told him he'd be kidnapping a senator's daughter. As much as Seth owed his old friend, he'd have balked at grabbing Levi McCord. Hell, there was talk the senator planned to run for president. Only a fool would abduct a senator's and possible future president's daughter.

All Wally had said was that Seth was to pick her up pronto. He'd assumed she was either trouble— or in trouble. Well, Levi McCord was obviously both. And now Seth Gantry was in a heap of trouble, as well.

Levi leaned back against the seat, clearly not believing anything he told her and yet expecting him to keep trying.

He drove for a few miles, grousing to himself. What did Senator McCord's daughter know about needing money, anyway? She came from a completely different world than he did. So where did she get off judging him because he took a job and was going to get paid well for it? She'd probably never worked a day in her life.

So she sure as hell wouldn't understand why he'd done as Wally asked without questioning him. And Seth had no intention of trying to explain it to her, even if he'd been able to.

"Why would he call *you?*" she demanded.

"I told you, we're friends, he trusts me. And he called me probably because I was close to where you were."

"Are you…trained for this sort of thing?"

"Yeah," he said indignantly. "I was a private investigator. Now I own a security business in Austin."

She studied him for a moment. "Let's say I believe you," she said, her voice suddenly soft and slightly more Southern. Almost…sweet.

He liked her rough-and-tough, direct approach better; at least he knew what to expect.

"How do you know you didn't kidnap—"

He shot her a warning look.

She mugged a face at him. "—grab the wrong woman?"

"Wally told me exactly where you'd be earlier this afternoon. He gave me everything from the stretch of road you'd be on and when, to your hair color and height, right down to the car you'd be driving. All I had to do was pick you up. A plane would be waiting nearby." Easy money. And he owed Wally. Seth always paid his debts.

"Then Wally had to know who I was and that *he* was breaking the law."

Seth figured so, but he didn't like the way she put it. "Wally is the most honest, law-abiding person I know. Believe me, he had a good reason for what he had me do." Seth refused to even consider the possibility that political enemies of Senator McCord's had tricked Wally. Wally was too smart for that. But this sure felt like the big league, so who knew who was behind it.

Levi let out a long sigh, as if he had to be the most gullible person she'd ever met. Or the stupidest. Or both. She seemed to shift mental gears, taking another tack. "When did he call you?"

"This morning."

"This morning?" she echoed. "What did he say?"

"Just that he needed me to do him a favor, that it had to be discreet and quick. And that I should use whatever...methods were necessary. He said to consider the case a DTA."

She stared at him. "DTA?"

"Don't trust anyone."

She seemed to think about that for a moment. "Surely you were curious about who I was. Why didn't you check my purse?"

He hated to admit just how curious he'd been after he'd seen her, after he'd noted the resemblance to Shanna. "I couldn't find your purse, but I didn't have much time to look. Maybe it had fallen under the seat. But your car registration wasn't there, either."

"The registration is always in my car and I definitely had my purse," Levi assured him.

He wondered if someone could have taken her purse and the car registration out before he got to her. Someone who for whatever reason didn't want him to know who he was kidnapping. Picking up, he amended quickly to himself. This woman was starting to confuse him. Who was he kidding? Levi McCord had messed him up the moment he saw her step out from her car.

"When was the last time you saw your purse?" he asked.

She frowned. "When Natalie and I left the ranch, I think."

"You think? Did you buy gas or anything in San Antonio?"

She shook her head. "I thought my purse was on the passenger seat when I tried to call the ranch on the car phone a few minutes before—"

She stopped so abruptly he glanced over at her. She'd turned pale, her eyes round.

"What?" he demanded.

"How did you get the battery out of my car phone so I couldn't call the ranch?"

He shook his head. "Wasn't me."

"And you probably don't know what happened to my bodyguards, either."

He didn't like her tone. "I didn't even know you *had* bodyguards." He didn't know a lot of things, he realized. She was right. Someone had removed the battery from her phone. It was too convenient that she couldn't call the ranch for help. Someone had also disposed of her bodyguards. Seth had had a lot more help than he'd known about, but instead of reassuring him, it made him nervous.

He shot a look at her. She sat, biting her lower lip, looking scared and vulnerable. He knew the look. Any minute she'd start crying.

He didn't blame her. But he also knew the moment she did, he'd want to take her in his arms and reassure her. So much for keeping his distance when just the thought of taking this woman in his arms—

"You aren't going to cry, are you?" he asked, deciding insensitive was better than foolish.

She swallowed hard and turned to glare at him, her eyes shiny and soft as lavender silk. "No, I'm not going to give you the satisfaction of crying."

"Good, I hate it when women cry."

"I'll just bet you do." She was mad again. Wasn't that what he wanted?

They drove along in a strained silence for a few minutes.

"All right, let's say I believe you," she said, her eyes still shiny but the vulnerability hidden behind her usual tough-girl demeanor. He hoped that's where she kept it.

"Then you don't have a problem with me getting out at the first town and calling my father to come get me," she said with authority.

He didn't answer quick enough.

"That's what I thought," she snapped, eyes blazing. "But the least you could have done was come up with a better story."

He might be a fool, but he wasn't a liar. He laid into the brakes. The pickup slid down the wet pavement, cocked a little to the left.

It wasn't until the truck had come to a stop that he looked over at her. She had the handcuffed hand braced on the seat, the other on the dash between them. Her eyes were wide, but her gaze was steady as she looked at him as if he were a madman. If she only knew.

"You don't get it, do you?" he snapped. "I don't have to come up with *any* story. I was hired to bring you here. Maybe not by name, but certainly based on everything else. Let's not kid ourselves, someone took care of your car phone and your bodyguards. Someone burned up Wally's cabin. Maybe I'm going out on a limb here, but I think it's too much of a coincidence that we were supposed to be in that cabin. Someone also either knew about the canoe that Wally always kept by the river or suspected that we would head for the river."

She swallowed hard, her eyes huge. "What are you saying?"

"That *someone* knows too much about you and me and Wally. I think that same someone wants you dead. And me, too, it seems."

"That's ridiculous. I might have been kidnapped for money or political favors, but kill me? For what possible purpose?"

He shook his head.

"Do you know *anything?*" she demanded angrily.

He took his time answering. "I might not be the knight in shining armor that you'd have hoped for in a situation like this, princess, but I'm all you've got."

"What if I'd prefer to save myself instead of leaving my fate up to some…dull-armored dark knight?"

"You wouldn't last twenty-four hours on your own."

Her eyes narrowed. "How do I know I'll last twenty-four hours with you?"

"You don't." It was all he could do not to— Hell, he didn't know what he'd do if he put his hands on her. And to think at first she'd reminded him of Shanna. "Look, in spite of how you feel about me—or me about you—I'm going to do everything I can to keep you alive."

"How cavalier since you're the one who got me into this mess."

He got the pickup moving again for something to do with his hands, other than wring her neck. "Don't flatter yourself. I'm only keeping you alive to save my own hide. If anything happens to you,

I'm going to hang not only for kidnapping but murder.''

Damn, was he going to have to wrestle this woman to the ground before the night was over? And to think that he usually liked a little fight in a woman. He *did* like the sudden image of the two of them on the ground wrestling. He could just see it. It'd quickly escalate into a whole other situation. He shook his head, wrestling with *that* mental image as it collared his thoughts in a headlock, painfully reminding him how long it had been.

He shifted gears, getting the truck cooking again, getting his mind back on track. The Boulder River cut through the mountains, leaving rocky cliffs on each side and a swath of fertile river bottom dotted with tall bare-limbed cottonwoods and snowcapped pines. The windshield wipers clacked back and forth and snow fell dense and white from out of the low clouds.

Levi had curled in the corner again, frowning into the snowstorm. Probably planning her next attack. Or maybe, like him, she was starting to realize that there wasn't any way he could have abducted her without help from someone who knew her. Someone who wanted both of them dead.

The question was who?

Chapter Five

Levi watched the snowy countryside flash by in the headlights, too shell-shocked to know what to believe. Too much had happened. Too much she couldn't explain. Or understand.

But what bothered her most was that she was starting to believe Seth. She almost felt sorry for pulling the gun on him, kicking him, taking the pickup and trying to throw him off the running board. Almost. She smiled at the memory of him sprawled facedown in the barn, the look of surprise on his face when he realized he'd been had—by her—again. It made her feel a little better since she'd foolishly let him take the pistol from her.

She stared out into the storm. Someone was trying to kill her. She desperately wanted to believe it was a mistake. Nor could she understand how he could have pulled off this kidnapping by himself. Well, not completely by himself.

She had a sudden flash of a woman with red hair getting up from the middle of the road beside a downed motorcycle.

"I just remembered something," she said, looking over at Seth. "The redhead on the bike."

"Jerilyn Ryers is my partner in the security business."

She shot him a look. "I thought this Wally person told you not to trust anyone?"

"Jerilyn knows even less than I do about this," he said a little too defensively. "She wouldn't have been there last night except she was worried and followed me. She suggested the motorcycle stunt because she thought I could use her help."

"How sweet. She just agreed to help you kidnap someone without knowing any of the details?" It seemed blind loyalty ran rampant around this cowboy. The depth of Seth's loyalty to his friends was nothing short of amazing. If Natalie called her tomorrow to ask her to pick up a pizza, no questions asked, Levi wasn't sure she would do it.

"Jerilyn trusts me," Seth said simply. "She's my partner."

Partner, my behind. "She trusts you, you trust her. And you both trust Wally. With all that trust going around, doesn't it seem strange that someone is trying to kill us?"

"Look, Jerilyn doesn't know Wally and he's never met her. She knew I was upset after Wally's call. She was worried about me and followed me to make sure I was all right."

"What are *partners* for, right?" Levi said. Why the mere thought of Seth's redheaded partner aggravated her, she didn't know. Probably because the woman had helped in Levi's not-exactly-kidnapping.

Seth let out a long perturbed sigh. "I don't expect you to believe this or understand, but three years ago I hired Jerilyn because she was down on her luck and because I'd been there enough times—"

He waved a hand through the air. "The point is, a year after that, she came into some money and bought into my company at a time when I really needed help. We're partners. Understand?"

"Perfectly." She tried to picture the redhead and couldn't. But she'd wager Seth's partner was a looker and there was a lot more to their relationship than business partners. "She must be good on a bike," Levi commented.

"She used to race professionally."

A woman of many talents. Levi groaned to herself. What did she care if the woman trusted this man so explicitly that she'd lay down her bike, even her life, for him? The woman might be a fool. Probably was.

Levi could feel his gaze on her and realized he'd asked her a question.

"Look, if you have any information, you'd better give it to me now."

She nodded, wondering what kind of help she could give him.

"Tell me everything you can remember about earlier today," he said. "Anyone who might have said or done anything…odd or out of character."

Thanksgiving dinner seemed like a long time ago. She stared out the windshield, thinking about her father's lie. Did it have something to do with her kidnapping? Of course not.

"*Everything*," Seth said, seeming to read her mind. "I assume you were on your way to your father's ranch outside of Vaquero or you wouldn't have been on that back road, right?"

"The Altamira isn't my father's ranch," she snapped, and immediately realized the ranch *was* her father's, even though he had no interest in it any-more. "*I* work the ranch."

He lifted one dark brow in surprise.

What did he think? That she didn't work at all?

"Then you live on the ranch?"

She nodded and looked away. Her father had wanted her to do something more...feminine. A Texas cattle ranch was men's work, he'd said. But after college, ranching was the only thing that inter-ested her. She knew her father had hoped she'd marry and give him grandchildren. How was she going to meet someone when she hardly ever left the ranch, he'd often lamented.

But then she didn't understand his love of politics any more than he understood her love of ranching.

"So tell me about Thanksgiving." Seth's dark eyes bored into her. "Don't leave out anything, no matter how small or seemingly irrelevant."

She hugged herself, wanting to argue that none of what was happening to her had anything to do with the Altamira or Thanksgiving or her family. But while she still knew next to nothing about this man, she realized she was starting to trust him—and his instincts.

So she told him about her father calling Sheriff Richards out to the house and the events that led up to her abduction. Her last clear memory was of see-ing the biker in the middle of the road, the red hair, and realizing it was a woman.

But after that, everything became fuzzy. She frowned as something tugged at her, nagging at her to remember as if it were important. But as hard as she tried, it still eluded her.

"It seems pretty obvious that someone disabled

Natalie's car, knowing I would give her a ride back into town,'' she said after a moment.

Seth nodded. ''Disabled her car, took care of your security guards, removed the battery from your car phone and got rid of your car registration and maybe even your purse.''

If Seth hadn't taken the battery out of her phone—and how could he have—then— ''Could it have been Wally?''

''Believe me, Levi, it wasn't Wally.''

Levi. That was the second time he'd called her that. The first time he'd been threatening to do who knows what to her, and her name had sounded alien on his tongue. But this time it sounded almost intimate. She liked the sound of her name on his lips.

She looked out at the falling snow and thought about Texas, the ranch and her father. If only she could talk to him. She didn't know what to believe. She'd always trusted her own intuition, but Seth was like a magnet, screwing up her compass. Confusing her.

She contemplated him. Her kidnapper—and her protector? She found herself wondering about this man. What did she know about Seth Gantry? Nothing really. He was a stranger. She knew he was stubborn. Stubbornly loyal. Look how determined he was that this Wally person hadn't betrayed him. She found herself hoping he was right, for his sake. She suspected he'd been disillusioned enough in his life already, though she wondered what made her think that.

He was also stubbornly secretive about himself. Why was that, she wondered.

She watched him rub his stubbled jaw, deep in

thought. He looked even more like a dark knight with a day's growth of beard. Someone equally dangerous as whoever was after them? Maybe more dangerous, she thought, remembering the way he'd fought the man who'd attacked them by the river. So why did that intensity reassure her rather than scare her? Because maybe he was just the type of man she needed right now. If he really was on her side.

The answers to Seth Gantry were here, she thought, looking out at the dark, snowy Montana landscape, unable to get a feel for it any more clearly than for the cowboy beside her.

But Seth was right. He and the redhead couldn't have pulled off the kidnapping by themselves, as talented as they were. They'd needed inside information. So whom did that leave? Someone at the ranch had to have helped.

AS SETH DROVE THROUGH the darkness and the snow, he turned everything over in his mind like one of those impossible cube puzzles, telling himself that he was letting Levi distract him because he didn't want to believe he'd been set up or what it all meant.

"If you let me call my father," she said after a few minutes had passed, "I can explain everything to him. I'm sure he'll—"

Seth laughed. This woman just didn't know when to give up. He couldn't help but feel a grudging admiration for her spirit, if not her foolhardiness.

"How can I expect your father to believe me when *you* don't even believe me?" he asked reasonably.

Amazingly she didn't argue. She bit her lower lip

as if considering that, calling attention to her mouth. He felt a stirring deep within him that had nothing to do with wrestling or throttling the woman or keeping the two of them alive.

The snowfall stopped as abruptly as it had started the moment they drove out of the mountains. Seth could see the lights of Big Timber ahead. Hopefully no one would be looking for them this far from the cabin yet. But he didn't kid himself that the guy by the canoe wouldn't soon alert his boss that they'd escaped down river. Word would be out that they were alive—and on the run. Someone would be looking for them. Soon.

"I need you on my side, Levi." He looked over at her, his expression softening. "I don't want to find myself looking down the barrel of a pistol with you behind it again, if I can help it. What do I have to do to prove to you that you can trust me?"

"Let me call my father."

He said nothing as the old pickup rumbled across the bridge and into the small western town.

"I expected more trees," she said, looking around.

"Used to be some big cottonwoods along the river, I guess, the biggest in the state."

"What happened to them?"

He shrugged. "I heard Lewis and Clark named this spot Big Timber because it was where they found trees large enough to make the log rafts they needed."

She scowled. "They name the town Big Timber, then cut down all the timber? What kind of sense does that make?"

He could relate to her need to make sense of

things. It was what had gotten him into private investigation work with Wally in the first place. A need for order. A need for justice and fairness. That need to make sense of a world gone crazy.

Well, it had just gone crazy again and, for the life of him, he couldn't make sense of it. Why in God's name had Wally asked him to steal Senator McCord's daughter? Seth knew there wasn't any way that Wally couldn't have known who she was. So where did that leave Seth?

Up a creek. Or in this case, down a river. Without a paddle. Or a clue.

He drove across town. It didn't take long. The town was small and dead this time of the night, except for a couple of farm trucks parked in front of the Grand Hotel.

A tumbleweed cartwheeled in front of the pickup's headlights at the edge of town. Seth pulled over by a pay phone next to a closed Conoco station, wanting to put more distance between them and the cabin and whoever would eventually come after them, but he couldn't wait any longer to talk to Wally. He didn't like what his gut instinct kept telling him—that any way Seth turned it, this felt like an inside job and he was the fall guy.

"I want you to come with me while I call Wally," he told Levi. He had to leave the truck running and he couldn't chance that she'd figure out some way, even handcuffed, to take off again. Keeping her alive meant keeping her with him whether she liked it or not. Or whether he liked it or not.

To his surprise, she didn't argue. Even when he handcuffed her to him and insisted she share the tiny outdoor booth with him. It was cozy with both of them snuggled in against the glass and each other.

The grimy phone booth windows instantly steamed up from their wet clothing. He told himself they wouldn't be such easy targets that way. Of course, they also couldn't see if anyone was sneaking up on them. He opened the door to clear the glass, not liking the idea of being sitting ducks.

But this wouldn't take long and he wasn't about to uncuff her. He couldn't be sure what she'd do. He hoped he'd convinced her, true or not, that he was her best hope to ever see Texas again, but you never knew with women.

He glanced at his watch. Three minutes to eleven. He dialed Wally's home number. After four rings, the answering machine picked up and Wally's voice instructed him to leave a message. He hung up without doing so and tried Wally's office. Another answering machine picked up. Seth hung up. No Wally. Why wasn't he surprised?

He stood for a moment, looking down at Levi.

"Can't reach him?" she asked, obviously even less surprised than he.

Seth leaned against the glass of the phone booth, weighing his options. What options? He took the phone and dialed, needing to hear a friendly voice. "Jerilyn?"

"Seth?" She sounded surprised. No, shocked. He heard her plop down, the chair creaking as she dropped into it.

"You sound surprised." He listened while she lit a cigarette and took a long drag, something she always did when she was nervous or upset.

She cursed softly. "You scared the hell out of me.

I got a call tonight, someone saying that you'd kidnapped Senator McCord's daughter and the two of you had been killed in an explosion.''

Whoever had set that firebomb had been so sure he and Levi had been killed that he'd called Jerilyn? That kind of confidence scared Seth. But that didn't fit with a professional hit. Professionals wouldn't have made that kind of mistake.

"Really?" he said to Jerilyn. "Any idea who the call was from?"

"Obviously some lunatic," she said. "You're too smart to kidnap a potential president's daughter."

Oh, sure.

"Nor did you get killed," she added unnecessarily.

Came close though. Too close. "You didn't recognize the voice or get the number on caller ID?" he asked.

"It was blocked."

Big surprise. "Did the caller say anything else? Like why he called *you* with this news?"

"Yeah," she said slowly, obviously noting that he hadn't yet denied kidnapping Olivia McCord. "He said the truth would come out about the armored car robbery and that I wasn't to worry because he knew I wasn't involved. Seth, is there anything you want to tell me?"

Seth bit back a curse and glanced at Levi. She was studying him intently in the light of the phone booth. The last thing he wanted was for her to learn that he'd been hired to protect an armored car full of money and that he'd screwed up, the money had been stolen and the robbery was still unsolved.

"I wish I knew what to tell you," he said to Jer-

ilyn, regretting her involvement in grabbing Levi—
even though Jerilyn's part had been her own idea.
This was much bigger than he'd suspected. But what
bothered him most was why the caller had men-
tioned the armored car robbery. What did that have
to do with any of this?

"Are you all right?" she asked.

"As good as can be expected." He took a deep
breath. She hadn't asked where he was or if he had
Levi or even if there was any truth to the caller's
accusation. Like him, she must suspect the line
could be tapped.

"Let's just treat this like any standard DTA," he
said, and hung up the phone.

"What did she say?" Levi asked impatiently.

He told her about the mysterious phone call, ed-
iting out the part about the armored car robbery.

"You have to let me call my father and tell him
I'm alive and safe," she said the moment he'd finished.

Seth studied her, surprisingly unsure of what to
do next. It was an alien feeling for him. He'd been
trained to react—and quickly. But right now he felt
he'd fallen headfirst into quicksand.

"Please," she said quietly, her eyes shiny. "My
father will get this all straightened out."

As if one phone call could do that. "Look, I think
calling the ranch could be a mistake," he said simply.

She shook her head, as if refusing to hear it. She
reached for the receiver with her free hand.

Seth sighed, covered her hand, and held it gently
but firmly. "Since we don't know who took the battery out of your car phone or who provided the exact

information on where you'd be this afternoon or who took care of your bodyguards, I say we don't trust anyone. You seem to think you can trust your father.''

Her eyes darkened. "Of course."

"Of course." The guy was a politician, that was ample reason to make Seth distrust him, but Seth was smart enough not to share his thoughts with Levi. "Give it your best shot, but I'm listening in. You talk to the senator. No one else. Understood? And don't mention my name."

He could see she didn't like being bossed around. Too bad. He was used to giving orders and not having to explain himself. So was she, it seemed.

He waited until she finally nodded her agreement to his conditions before he released her hand. He knew she thought she'd get her father on the line and that this would be over, just as Seth had hoped when he'd dialed Wally's number. Maybe she'd have better luck than he'd had, but he doubted it.

"I'll be listening," he warned as he held the phone while she dialed with her free hand. "Don't tell anyone where we are. Not even your father. You have no idea who else might have access to the line."

He could tell she thought he was just being paranoid. Damn straight.

The phone rang several times before it was picked up. "McCord residence," a woman said.

He watched her frown. She didn't recognize the voice.

"This is Levi, let me speak to my father."

"Who is this?" the woman at the other end of the line asked.

"Olivia McCord."

A man's voice came on the line. "Levi?"

"Daddy!"

"Oh, thank God. You're all right?"

"Yes." Tears welled in her eyes. "Then you heard what happened?" She swallowed and looked up at Seth. "That I've been kidnapped?"

"I'm sorry, honey, I had no choice. Is Gantry there with you?"

She stared at Seth, seemingly speechless. "*You* had me kidnapped, Daddy?"

Seth took the phone from her hand. "Senator? Would you like to tell me just what the hell is going on?"

Chapter Six

"You saved my daughter's life, Mr. Gantry," a cultured, Southern male voice said. "I am very thankful. Wally was right about you. Is he there? I'd like to talk to him."

"So would I, but he seems to be missing." Seth tried hard to rein in his anger. "Wally didn't meet us at the airstrip tonight as planned. Nor at his cabin. Which is just as well, since someone blew it up, thinking your daughter and I were inside."

"Oh, my God," McCord exclaimed. "They found out that you were meeting Wally? There *is* a leak at the ranch then. Levi's all right, isn't she?"

Seth looked down at her. "She's scared and apparently with good reason. I guess this is her first kidnapping."

"It couldn't be helped," McCord said.

Seth closed his eyes and counted silently to ten. He hated coming in in the middle of a movie; he really hated being the star of the production and not even knowing he'd gotten the role. "Senator, I want some answers and I want them now."

"Of course," McCord said, sounding shaken. "I got a call from Wally early this morning. He had discovered a murder plot involving my daughter. At first, I thought I could protect her at the ranch with the help of local law enforcement and my own security men, but Wally insisted we get her out of Texas as quickly as possible." Before Seth could ask, the senator added, "Wally and I became friends after he did some investigative work for me years ago."

"A murder plot?" Seth asked. "He wasn't any more specific than that?"

"He said it involved someone he knew, but he didn't elaborate. He warned me to trust no one, except you. I told him to do what he had to do and get back to me. But I haven't heard from him since around nine tonight. He called to tell me that you had my daughter and that he was meeting the two of you at the airstrip."

Seth swore under his breath. The airstrip. Not the cabin. So when had the plans changed? Had Wally changed them, or someone else?

"I understand why Wally didn't tell me the specifics," Seth said, "but you could have told your daughter that you'd hired someone to kidnap her."

The senator sighed. "You've become acquainted with my daughter. Do you really think I could have persuaded her to leave the ranch on her own with a total stranger based on an old friend of mine's say-so?"

"She *is* a little headstrong," Seth agreed.

Levi glared at him, making him nervous. He couldn't help but think of Shanna and how much Levi had reminded him of her at first. Although now he was struck more by the dissimilarities, he still couldn't shake off that feeling of déjà vu—and doom.

"I suggest you send someone for your daughter," he told the senator. "Obviously it isn't any safer for her up here than it was in Texas. Maybe even less so."

Several beats of silence answered him. Then McCord said slowly, "I'm afraid that's not possible. It would appear we have a leak at the Altamira and until I find out who is involved, she won't be safe, especially here." Seth could tell admitting there was a traitor in his midst came hard to him. McCord sounded like a man who inspired loyalty not betrayal, much like his daughter, Seth suspected.

"One other thing," the senator added. "Wally didn't want the FBI or local law enforcement up there involved, either. He said he had his reasons."

No cavalry, Seth thought. Just him and Levi. He pressed his fingers against his temple, that feeling of déjà vu a bad headache now. "Do you realize what you're asking?"

"Yes, Mr. Gantry, I'm asking you to find out who's behind this at your end while I try to find the leak at my ranch. Wally didn't trust my daughter's safety to anyone but you. He must have had his reasons. So I'm putting my faith in you, too."

All this flattery was going to his head. "No offense, Senator, but you don't even know me."

"I know you've saved my daughter's life twice."

"Senator, there are things about me—" Seth wanted to argue that, with the senator's resources, why trust one man, especially him. But how could Seth be certain that the men the senator sent would keep Levi safe? And it wasn't as though he could just walk away from all of this.

"Check in with me every day," the senator said in a tone that made it clear, at least for him, the subject was closed. "Call this number," he rattled off a phone number, "and leave a message. Don't call the ranch again, because I won't be monitoring the line after this. Now, may I speak to my daughter?"

Seth could tell Levi was just as anxious to speak to her father. He handed her the phone and stood watching her, listening just to her end of the conversation, which wasn't much. The senator was doing most of the talking, Levi only listening, wide-eyed.

"I understand, Daddy. You did what you thought you had to do, but I'm not a child. You should have told me—" She looked at the ceiling and sucked in a long breath. "Yes." She flicked a glance at Seth. "All right." She listened for a few uninterrupted moments, although Seth could tell it was hard for her. Then her voice and her face softened and her eyes shone with tears. "I love you, too. I will. You be careful too."

She hung up the phone and looked at Seth with eyes the color of liquid lavender, soft and inviting as hell. A man could lose himself in those eyes, he thought, dragging his gaze away. He was in enough trouble without that.

"My father had me kidnapped," she said numbly, sounding still a little shocked by the turn of events.

Seth nodded, not any happier than she was about it. But the senator was right about one thing: Wally wouldn't have involved Seth if he hadn't had his reasons. It was those reasons that bothered Seth the most. He had to find Wally.

"Memorize this number," he said to Levi, and repeated the phone number the senator had given him. "If something should happen to me, call it." But he feared if something happened to him, she wouldn't be making any phone calls.

LEVI STOOD in the phone booth, shaken and stunned, her mind racing. Her own father had had her kidnapped because of a threat against her. Well, at least it explained her father's behavior earlier today. His lying to Sheriff Richards. His talk about an impromptu vacation. He must have realized the sheriff or a vacation wouldn't be enough. She knew her father and the extremes he'd go to to keep his family safe. She couldn't really blame him under the circumstances, but she still had trouble accepting it.

And it certainly changed things with Seth.

She watched him push open the phone booth door and look out. At this late hour, the town of Big Timber was as dark and quiet as a morgue. A morgue? Where had that come from? Nothing about Big Timber looked menacing. But she knew now that she wasn't safe. Not here. Not in Texas. Hadn't Seth been trying to tell her that all along? "I owe you an apology."

"You owe me nothing," he said, not looking at her.

She couldn't leave it at that. He'd saved her life. And she'd made it as difficult for him as she could. "If you hadn't done what you did—"

"That's all water under the bridge." He turned to meet her gaze, his eyes dark and soft in the light of the phone booth. "Unfortunately, your life is still in danger."

Down the street, she heard an engine groan as what sounded like a large truck came around the corner. A set of headlights washed over the phone booth, catching Seth standing outside. He quickly stepped back into the booth and closed the door.

"What's wrong?" she asked as the glare of the headlights filled the phone booth, exposing them. The truck slowed.

Seth swore.

"Do you think it's them?" she cried.

"Quiet!"

"But they couldn't know we got out of the cabin. Not yet, could they?" she whispered.

He looked down at her. "Damn, is there no way to shut you up?"

Before she knew what he intended to do, he wrapped his free arm around her and pulled her into him, his mouth lowering to hers. Her lips parted in surprise at the kiss, at the warmth of his lips, the wonderful softness of his mustache, the comforting strength of his arm around her.

She didn't even hear the truck speed up and disappear down the street.

It wasn't until Seth drew back, leaving her leaning against the glass with her heart pounding, her pulse racing, her eyes still closed and her mouth open, that she realized just how caught up in the kiss she'd been.

"The truck's gone now," she heard Seth say softly. Was that strangled amusement in his voice?

She opened her eyes and wanted to strangle *him*.

There was amusement, surprise and something else she wasn't sure she liked in his expression. Regret?

It was also very clear that the kiss had been nothing more to him than a ploy to divert the attention of the driver of the truck that had gone by—and shut her up.

Levi pushed herself off the glass, trying to look as unaffected by his kiss and as dignified as possible. She stumbled into him.

"Are you all right?" he asked, catching her.

"Just tripped over your big feet," she said, angry with him for kissing her, for making her feel something, for looking as though he wished he hadn't kissed her. She pulled free of his grasp, but they were still joined by the handcuffs. "Don't you think it's time you took these stupid things off me?"

He studied her for a long moment, then reached into his pocket and, with the key, unlocked the handcuff from his wrist, but not hers. "We still have some things we need to discuss."

She looked at him in disbelief. "Such as?" So help him, if he apologized for kissing her—

"About that kiss—"

"Don't you dare apologize for kissing me." She snatched the key from his hand and unlocked the handcuff around her wrist. Then she dropped both into his hand. "Are we going to wait for that truck to come back or are we getting out of here?"

He actually smiled. "We're getting out of here."

She squeezed past him and stalked to the pickup.

"I wasn't going to apologize for kissing you," he said as he joined her in the cab of the pickup.

"Good." She stared out into the night while he pulled away from the phone booth. What had he been going to say, she wondered. But she wasn't about to ask, nor let on that she'd enjoyed the fool kiss and even its aftereffects.

Seth drove out of town, leaving the lights of Big Timber glittering behind them.

"Where are we going?" she asked, after they'd gone a few miles and she felt anchored again.

"Livingston. To find Wally."

She saw him glance in his rearview mirror as a set of headlights appeared behind them. "Did you get a look at the truck that went by the phone booth?"

"A red stock truck, Park County plates."

She'd had her eyes closed when the truck passed and nothing on her mind but Seth's kiss. Good thing one of them was paying attention. So why wasn't she pleased by his answer?

"My father thinks there's a leak at the ranch," she said, changing the subject.

Seth nodded. "He wants me to keep you up here in Montana and safe until he can find the leak. Until I figure it out at this end."

"*We* figure it out."

He shook his head at her. "This is one of the things we have to get straight. While I don't have a lot of choice, since we're in this together, we're going to have to agree to some ground rules." He considered her for a moment. "You have to do as I say."

"Sure," she said, hoping that appeased him. "After all, you're the trained professional, right?"

The man was no fool. He glanced over at her, unsureness on his face.

Good. She wasn't all that sure about him, either.

After all, what did she know about Seth Gantry? Nothing, except that he could fight, paddle a canoe, hot-wire a car and kiss. Not much to stake her life on.

No, if he thought she was going to sit back idly through this, he was dead wrong. After all, someone was after *her* not him, right? And she liked to think she could take care of herself.

She just hoped they'd be able to find Wally and get this over with as quickly as possible. *If* Wally had the answers. She knew Seth was worried that something had happened to his friend. So was she.

But Wally wasn't her only concern as she and Seth headed for Livingston. It was Seth. He'd intrigued her—even before the kiss—but he also worried her.

She'd never gone into anything blindly. Just the opposite. She took her time making decisions, weighing all her options, considering all the variables. That was probably why she'd never fallen head over heels in love. Only fools did that, right?

As she looked over at the cowboy next to her, she knew she was going into this blindly. But what else could she do? Her father had told her to trust Seth Gantry.

Unfortunately, that did little to reassure her. Her father had never met the cowboy. And what James Marshall McCord didn't realize—and Levi did— was that Seth was exactly the kind of man her father had always warned her about.

Ahead, the highway trailed the winding ribbon of river west. She caught glimpses of rocky bluffs and tall pines backed by towering snowcapped peaks that glowed in the moonlight.

The country would have normally stolen her attention, but instead Seth did that. She watched him staring out at the landscape with a look so close to love it made her ache.

"It's pretty," she commented, hoping to draw him out.

He smiled, probably anticipating where she was headed.

"So why did you leave and go to Texas?" she asked, not wanting to disappoint him.

"It's a long story." He shook his head as he glanced over at her. "Remind me to tell you my entire life story someday."

She could tell he was being facetious, but she was dead serious. "I'll hold you to that."

He chuckled. "I don't doubt you will."

What had happened to make him leave? She could see it in his face, feel it in her heart. There was a pain there, a deep sorrow. It made her even more curious about the man, because she knew that kind of pain usually had something to do with a woman.

As the pickup rumbled across a narrow bridge, she found herself staring down at the water, seeking the answer in the ice-edged, dark green. In the meantime, she warned herself to be wary of him. Getting too close would be a mistake. His kiss had proved that.

She jumped at the sound of Seth's low curse and turned to find him staring into the rearview mirror. "What is it?"

"I think we're being followed."

Chapter Seven

"Don't look back," Seth ordered.

But of course Levi ignored him. "All I can see are headlights," she said, turning in the seat to stare behind them. "You think it's the red stock truck you saw in Big Timber?"

"Maybe." He'd been watching his rearview mirror and keeping an eye on all the cars and trucks that passed them. Considering that the old Harvester pickup pegged at forty-five, everyone had passed them, making him wish he'd stolen a little faster rig in Big Timber.

But he'd wanted to get out of town as quickly as possible, the old Harvester was nondescript and hopefully whoever was after them would expect him, with his court-documented talents, to be able to steal a better rig than this.

And the truth was, his mind had been on other things. At the time, kissing Levi had seemed like a perfectly reasonable thing to do. It had also worked: the truck driver had slowed, must have seen them lip-locked and then driven on. And it *had* shut Levi up.

So why was he so upset with himself for kissing her?

Damned if he knew.

He glanced back again at the lights of a truck. coming up behind them. In the moonlit night, it looked like the same one he'd seen in Big Timber.

"What are our options?" Levi asked.

"Options?" He glanced over at her, not at all surprised by the stubborn set of her jaw or the determination burning in her eyes. She was a woman who was up to a good fight. He realized he liked that about her a lot.

"Can we lose him?" she asked, and met his gaze.

He raised a brow. "In this? You've got to be kidding."

"I thought you private-eye types were good at this sort of thing."

He shook his head at her. "You watch too much television." In the rearview mirror he could see the stock truck bearing down on him. Just ahead was the first exit into Livingston. A few more minutes and the stock truck would catch them.

At the last minute, he let the exit go past, watching the side of the road ahead for the right spot. Just as the stock truck's grill filled his rearview mirror, Seth yelled, "Hang on!" and jerked the wheel hard to the right. The Harvester rattled off the pavement, down into the ditch, bumping along through tall summer-dried grass and weeds and several snowdrifts, then up onto the old highway leading into Livingston.

He looked back to see the stock truck's brake lights flash bright red. It took the driver a while to get the larger truck stopped. He began backing up to the exit.

Seth had bought them only minutes. He glanced over at Levi. She was grinning at him.

"Not bad," she commented.

It sounded like high praise to his ears as he floored the Harvester and got it up to 47 mph.

"What in the world?" Levi cried.

He glanced up from the speedometer expecting to see a roadblock. Instead it was only the microskyline smudged gritty brown in the lights of town. The first gust hit the pickup, rocking it as the already pitiful pickup's paint job was showered with pea-sized gravel.

Seth had almost forgotten about the wind. "Welcome to Livingston, one of the windiest places on earth."

A tattered flag stood straight out in what had to be a near gale-force windstorm. Airborne dust, dirt and gravel eclipsed not only the road in front of him, but most of the town and the mountains around it for a few moments.

"Tonight the wind might actually work in our favor," he said, glancing back to see the stock truck still a speck in the distance, but gaining quickly.

Seth followed the wide set of train tracks into the old railroad town. Livingston hadn't changed much in the eight years he'd been gone. At just the sight of it, he felt a rush of emotions assault him. Home.

Fortunately, he didn't have time to take any trips down memory lane.

He hung a left down a gravel street that dropped toward the river, then a right, another left. Running out of street at the river, he turned right, the air a gritty brown haze against the patches of snow that hadn't already blown away. Ahead he could make out the dulled glow of neon. Downtown Livingston.

Somehow, he'd expected it to look different. The fact that it didn't seemed to make coming home all that much worse. He tried to tell himself it was just like any other small, windblown, dusty western town in Montana. There were dozens of them in the state.

But it was lie. There was no place like Livingston. The downtown area with its cafés and clothing stores, bars and banks wasn't more than four blocks square at its center. And it wasn't much to look at, either, even with the fancy fishing and outdoors shops, art galleries and high-priced restaurants.

What made Livingston different wasn't just that the Yellowstone River, one of the most famous trout-fishing rivers in the world, ran through it. It was the way the town sat in the palm of the mountains. And that it had been *his* town, *his* river. His home.

He'd known coming back would be hard. Just not this hard. And not like this. Scared and on the run. The black sheep of the family returns—in trouble. Some things never change.

He rounded a corner, pulled down a narrow, dark alley and parked between a couple of pickups.

"This is where we get out," he said and, taking Levi's hand, pulled her after him. He ducked into the back door of a cowboy bar, the air filled with loud country music, the smell of stale beer and cigarette smoke, the cacophony of dozens of conversations.

With Levi's hand still in his, he drew her through the packed bar. The regulars turned with small-town curiosity as Seth and Levi pushed their way through the crowd. Seth felt like a stranger in his own hometown. After everything that had happened, maybe he was and always would be.

Once outside on the main drag, he and Levi raced across the street in the dark to the narrow park that skirted the railroad tracks beside the old depot. He stopped running and pulled Levi into a wedge of deep shadow beside the huge stone building, shielding her with his body from the wind and the cold.

Somewhere in the distance he heard a church bell chime out twelve. Midnight in Livingston, Montana. It was a lonely, desolate sound that reminded him how dangerous his homecoming was.

"You certainly know your way around this place," Levi noted quietly.

He smiled to himself. Subtle, this woman wasn't. "I used to live here."

"Really?"

He felt her gaze on him and knew she was waiting for more. "It's my hometown. I grew up around here."

It was time to get moving again, and not just to keep Levi from grilling him about his past. He glanced at his watch. Five minutes had passed and no sign of the stock truck. Seth had pretty much decided that it had been a case of mistaken identity. The guy in the truck must have thought he recognized the old International Harvester pickup. Might have. Well, he and Levi wouldn't be driving it anymore anyway.

"Come on," he said, taking her gloved hand again. "We're going to walk."

The wind howled, whipping the trees along the

narrow street, sending the last of the leaves flying past as he led Levi toward the river.

"What about the pickup you stole?" she asked.

"It's too dangerous to drive it now and there really isn't a reason. We can walk anywhere in Livingston we want to go." He led her down a side street, avoiding the scarce street lamps and the moon, both dimmed by the clouds and the wind. It did feel as if another storm was blowing in.

"Where exactly is it we want to go?" she asked.

"Wally's house."

WALLY LIVED IN a small house set back in a stand of cottonwoods. The air smelled of river bottom, and through the mostly bare shifting branches, Seth could see the glimmer of the river, its wind-whipped surface a hammered silver.

He walked down the driveway, hoping he'd find Wally's van in the garage and Wally home, worry dogging his every step. He didn't like the fact that Wally wasn't answering his phone. He feared that something had happened to him.

Along with the worry were the memories. Shanna. She seemed to be everywhere, in the houses they passed, in the smells that blew up from the river, in the sound of the wind buffeting the trees.

And while Levi still reminded him a little of Shanna, the differences between the two women had become all the more apparent. Shanna had been reserved, demure, even timid. Levi was...well, Levi. There was nothing shy about her, nothing coy, nothing prissy. She was courageous, confident, defiant, strong and stubborn. All things that he couldn't help but like about her.

But at the same time, she possessed a feminine softness that made him feel protective whether she liked it or not. He could tell the woman had it in her head that she could take care of herself. While it worried him, he also liked that about her, too.

Wally's van wasn't in the garage. Seth could see mail sticking out of the mailbox beside the front door and two newspapers haphazardly tossed on the walk.

The night seemed darker as he led Levi around to the back and tapped at the door. He waited a moment, then tried the knob. The door opened. Not surprising. Did anyone in Livingston lock their doors? But still, he felt a deep sense of dread at what he'd find. He glanced over his shoulder.

"You might want to wait here," he said to Levi.

She shook her head. "I'm coming with you."

That didn't surprise him, either. "Try not to touch anything."

He flipped the switch, throwing a glare of gold across the living room.

Wally collected things. Not just things—people as well, and Seth was one of those people. The living room was an eclectic mix of auction and garage sale furniture, but it looked perfect in Wally's comfortable, warm home, from the moose head to the Navajo rugs on the walls.

Nothing looked out of place. Nor was there any sign of a struggle. The logs in the rock fireplace had burned down to ashes. The air had since grown cold.

Seth moved slowly through the small house. No dirty dishes in the sink. He felt the coffeepot. Cold. He opened the refrigerator but could tell nothing from the four cans of beer, a stick of pepperoni, a chunk of cheese starting to mold and a jar of mustard. Seth knew that Wally ate most of his meals out.

The washcloth in the bathroom, neatly folded over the towel rack, was dry. So was the tub.

The only hint that Wally had been here recently was the bedroom. A pair of jeans and a flannel shirt still lay over a wheelchair beside the bed. Under the wheelchair, worn cowboy boots rested against each other for support.

"Is the wheelchair Wally's?" Levi asked, obviously surprised.

He nodded as he stared at the boots and remembered the first time he'd met Wally. Before the wheelchair. Before Shanna. Back when Seth had been nothing more than a punk ranch kid who thought he knew more than he did. But Wally had changed that. Wally had taken him under his wing, taught him to be a private investigator. And ultimately, taught him about life.

"You didn't tell me he was in a wheelchair," she admonished. "If his wheelchair is here then—"

"This is just the small one he uses around the house," he said, still distracted by the past and the terrible feeling that history was about to somehow repeat itself.

Something on the wall caught her eye. He watched her move to the framed photograph.

"Is that Wally with you?" she asked.

He stepped closer, although he knew that particular photograph by heart. "Yes."

"Before he was in a wheelchair," Levi noted. "And the girl?"

"Wally's niece, Shanna." Seth supposed Shanna

did look like a girl in that photo; she'd just turned twenty-two when it was taken. Seth had been twenty-six. Ten years ago now.

He waited for Levi to say something about the resemblance between her and Shanna, but she studied the photo intently for a long moment without comment.

"She's pretty," Levi said at last as she turned to look at him.

He nodded, surprised that she hadn't seen the similarities that he saw so easily. Too easily. "Yeah." He looked away, but he knew she was frowning without even looking at her. Her violet eyes would be narrowed a little as if in intense concentration, her mouth puckered slightly, a small furrow between her perfect brows.

"Come on," he said quickly before she could ask another question, one he wouldn't want to answer. "There's nothing here."

ON THE CONTRARY, Levi thought as they left. The photograph of Seth smiling beside the young woman and the large stocky man, the three looking happy and close, felt like another piece of the Seth puzzle.

It was all she could do not to quiz him, but from the look on his face, she doubted she'd get anywhere. She knew a little something about heartbreak. Hers had been in college and more like a schoolgirl crush. But she knew the look and Seth had the look. This girl had broken his heart. Was Shanna also why Seth had left Montana, why he didn't want to talk about his reason for leaving?

So where was this Shanna now, Levi wondered as they stepped back out into the wind and darkness.

She huddled down in her coat, walking fast to keep up with Seth. She hoped they didn't run into Shanna, still in Livingston. Levi didn't want to have to see Seth go through that.

They passed quaint old houses with wide, railed porches and towering brick chimneys. She stole peeks into the houses with lights on. They looked warm and homey and pulled at her, making her ache for the lives of the people inside them.

The ache surprised her. She'd yearned for something for the past few years now. But until this moment, she hadn't wanted to put a name to that yearning. A husband. Children. A home of her own. Her family had always been her father, Robin and Mary; her home, the Altamira Ranch. Her father had always needed her. Still needed her. And so did the ranch, she reminded herself.

Her eyes teared, no doubt from the cold, and she wiped at them with her glove. Christmas lights blurred. She'd forgotten about the holidays. Even forgotten for a while that someone was trying to kill her.

But Seth suddenly reminded her. He pulled her down an alley, the wind spinning dust devils into the night and sending plastic garbage cans cartwheeling into the next county.

"Are we being followed again?" she asked, looking back, worried.

"I just don't want to take any chances," he said as he turned up the collar on his coat and kept moving.

Who was he afraid might see him? The bad guys? Or Shanna? Or someone else who knew him?

How many secrets did this man have anyway?

SETH WALKED HEAD DOWN into the wind, intent on movement as he tried not to think about what could have happened to Wally. Levi kept up, fighting the wind but walking quickly, silently.

It was half past midnight when they reached Wally's office, an old narrow four-story brick building. Seth noticed that, except for Wally's van, there were no cars in the small lot.

Seth glanced inside the van only to find it empty, then up at the building. He thought he saw movement in the dark window of Wally's fourth-floor office, but it could have just been a trick of the moonlight or the wind in the tree branches.

As he climbed the steps to the front entrance, the wind roared in the trees. In the distance, a train whistled as it passed through town, a low rumble. He tried the handle. Locked.

"Let's go around back." He was more comfortable with back entrances anyway.

Levi didn't seem to hear him. She stood, staring down the block, a wistful look on her face. He figured she was thinking about her own home and the mess she was in rather than the picturesque houses that lined the far side of the street.

Home. He'd once entertained the dream of owning a home. Something old, with a history, a sense of belonging. He'd even wanted it in town rather than on ranch land. But that had been eight years ago and because Shanna wanted to live in town. Now home was wherever he tossed his hat.

Getting into the back of Wally's building proved easy. Too easy. He'd planned to pick the lock but didn't have to. The door was standing ajar.

He felt the hair rise on his neck the moment he

stepped inside. Silence seemed to hunker in the hallways.

He glanced toward the elevator, then at the door marked Stairs and felt the weight of the pistol in his coat pocket. The elevator, he recalled, was old and loud. He didn't relish the idea of being boxed in something that would warn anyone upstairs that they were coming.

He pushed open the stairwell door and heard it. A thunk. Then another. He told himself it was probably someone who'd decided to work late or the janitor doing some late-night cleaning—until he remembered the empty parking lot. The sound chilled his blood.

He drew the gun and motioned for Levi to stay behind him as he started up the stairs. He could hear the sound above them and Levi right behind him.

The stairs wound up four stories with small landings on each floor. With an urgency he couldn't explain, he took the stairs two at a time. He was almost to the third-floor landing when he heard it again.

Only this was a different sound. One that seemed to be coming closer. *Clatter, clatter, clink.* Something large was tumbling down the stairs, headed this way.

Seth didn't see the object until it hit the third-floor landing, ricocheted off the wall and careened down the stairs toward them. A wheelchair.

Seth grabbed Levi and pulled her out of the way as the wheelchair banged past them. Now he could hear another sound, footfalls above him. He rushed up the stairs, fear a knot in his throat, the pistol gripped in his hand. Below him he heard Wally's wheelchair connect with the second-floor landing with a resounding clang that echoed up through the stairwell. Then silence.

Seth expected to find Wally in a heap somewhere along the steps as broken and battered as his wheelchair. But Seth reached the fourth-floor landing and still no Wally. No sound of footfalls, either. Directly across the hall, he could see Wally's office door standing slightly ajar. A shaft of thin light spilled out on the worn linoleum.

Seth slowed, softening his steps, and motioned for Levi to stay back.

LEVI STOOD ON THE LANDING, feeling exposed. She could feel a cold draft of air coming from somewhere and shivered, unable to throw off the image of the wheelchair tumbling down the stairs. Empty. She knew Seth had to be as scared as she was for his friend.

She watched Seth inch his way toward the doorway, the pistol ready. The silence seemed almost palpable, as if even the old building were holding its breath. In the cold, echoing silence, she could hear nothing but the pounding of her heart, the sound of her fear.

Seth reached the door and slowly pushed it all the way open. It creaked, making her jump. She let out a gasp. The office had been ransacked; file cabinets were turned over, folders and papers were strewn across the floor.

Seth stepped into the office and stood with his back to her for a long moment. Like her, he had to be worrying about Wally. And no doubt wondering where the person was who'd pushed the wheelchair down the stairs, who they'd heard running away just moments ago.

Seth turned and frowned. He pointed across the ransacked office to where a rear office door stood open. Through the second doorway she had a clear view of the elevator. The elevator was closed but the dial above it showed the car was still sitting on this floor.

Suddenly something clanked loudly deep in the building and groaned rebelliously into motion. The elevator! The car began to descend, the racket diminishing as it dropped.

At the initial sound, Seth raced past her and down the stairs. She watched the dial over the elevator move to three, then inch toward two. Below her, she could hear the clatter of Seth's footsteps, dying away, just like the sound of the elevator car, and knew he'd reach the ground floor before the doors had a chance to open.

Her fear for Seth froze her for a long moment, then she stepped toward Wally's office, knowing he had to be here somewhere. He couldn't have gone far without his wheelchair, could he?

But the office, while a mess, was too small to have any bodies lying around unnoticed.

She heard the elevator thunk to a stop and held her breath, waiting for the sound of the doors shuddering open and the possible explosion of gunfire.

That's when she heard it. Another sound, this one softer than the clank of the elevator. This one definitely closer. She turned as if in slow motion. Someone was behind her. Wally?

A closet door, hidden behind the full coatrack, creaked open and in that instant, a large figure dressed in a heavy coat and a ski mask burst out, knocking over the coatrack. The man moved so quickly she didn't have time to scream, let alone run. He grabbed her by the throat with two large gloved hands and slammed her into the desk, his hands tightening around her throat. She kicked at him as she fell back over the cluttered desk. He pinned her legs with his body as she tore at his gloved hands with her fingers, her lungs screaming for air. But he was too strong for her.

Darkness threatened at the edge of her sight as her hands felt around on the desk for a weapon. Her fingers latched onto a large stapler. Her other hand found a heavy book. The darkness closed in, and tiny lights danced at the edge of her vision. With nothing to lose, she brought both hands up at the same time, slamming the book and the stapler into the sides of his head.

The combined effect made him stumble back, loosening his hold on her throat and giving her room to get a boot up. She kicked with all her strength as she gasped for air, striking the man only in the arm.

To her surprise, he howled with pain, falling back over the mess he'd made on the floor, but he didn't go down. He caught himself and, holding his arm, charged her, anger in the gray eyes she could now see behind the mask. Anger and pain.

Levi flung herself to the far side of the desk away from him and opened her mouth, praying for enough air to get out at least one good scream before he reached her.

SETH HAD POSITIONED himself in front of the elevator on the ground floor, the pistol leveled at the doors when they finally clanged opened. He'd been so sure of what he'd find, that it took him a moment to realize what he was seeing. A man lay sprawled against the elevator wall by the controls in a pool of blood.

"Wally." Seth rushed forward and knelt over him. He hurriedly felt for a pulse. Weak, but still beating.

Wally's eyes flickered open, and he grabbed a handful of Seth's coat in his fingers and drew him farther down. A whisper of a word. Then Wally's hand dropped, his eyes closed.

Seth had to call for help. As he started to rise, fear washed over him. Levi. If the man who'd done this wasn't in the elevator—

His thought stopped dead as a scream tore through the building.

Chapter Eight

Seth shot to his feet, the scream echoing in his ears. He was running long before he hit the stairs, flying up them, his heart in his throat, the pistol in his hand.

Just as he reached the fourth-floor landing and could see Wally's open office doorway, he caught movement off to his left, but not before something struck his shoulder with a glancing blow. He stumbled back just in time to see a large dark figure hurl the wooden coatrack at him.

Seth dodged out of the way just an instant before the rack smacked into the wall next to him. In that instant, the figure darted past and down the stairs.

All Seth's training demanded he go after the attacker. But a stronger instinct sent him rushing into Wally's office, calling out her name. "Levi?"

Her head popped up from behind the desk at the sound of his voice. She looked as though she'd been through hell, her hair tangled, her cheek and neck red, scratched and starting to bruise, her shirt torn and hanging off one shoulder. He'd never seen a more wonderful sight.

He stepped through the debris around the desk

and pulled her into his arms, holding her tight as relief washed over him. She hugged him back with a strength that assured him she was all right, at least physically. But he could feel her shaking and knew it would be a while before she was really all right again.

"Are you okay?" he asked, pulling back a little, needing to find the phone and call an ambulance for Wally, but not wanting to let her go.

She nodded, biting her lower lip as she brushed at the fresh tears. "I'm just relieved to see you."

"Same here." As desperately as he wanted to hold her and dry those tears, there was no time. He looked around for the phone and saw it sticking out of a stack of file folders. "I found Wally." He dragged it out, plugged the line back into the wall and dialed 911. When he looked up, he found Levi staring wide-eyed at him.

"Is he...?"

"Alive," he answered, feeling as numb and scared as she looked. "Barely." When the emergency number answered, he requested an ambulance and gave the dispatcher the address.

"Did you get a look at the man?" Seth asked after he'd hung up the phone.

She shook her head. "He wore a ski mask." Like the man who'd attacked them by the canoe on the Boulder River. Only with this man, she knew she'd recognize his eyes if she ever saw them again. They were the gray eyes of a lunatic.

AFTER THE DOCTOR CHECKED Levi's throat and assorted bruises and scrapes, he pointed the way down the hospital hallway to Wally's room. She found

Seth standing beside a hospital bed, holding his friend's hand. Wally looked older and paler than the man she'd seen in the photograph with Seth and Shanna, but still a powerfully built man for his age and disability. His head was wrapped with a wide white bandage, and a series of tubes and wires ran from him to the machines beside the bed.

"How is he?" she asked softly as she entered the room.

Seth looked up. The lines of his face were drawn and his dark eyes worried. "How are *you?*" he asked in concern.

She gave him a thumbs-up. Her throat hurt, making it painful to talk, but she didn't mention it to Seth, knowing he'd probably see it as the only good thing that had come out of all this. "Has he regained consciousness?" she whispered.

Seth shook his head. "The doctors ran tests. They won't have the results for a while. But nothing seems to be broken. He lost quite a lot of blood from the head wound, but his pulse is stronger."

"That's good, right?" she asked hopefully.

Seth attempted a smile. "You sure you're all right?" He studied her, wondering if she was telling him everything. "The doc checked you out?"

She nodded. "Don't worry about me." She glanced down at Wally, then back up at Seth and saw the fear in his eyes. "What is it?"

He looked away. "Can't hide much from you."

"I'm too nosy."

"Wally woke for a moment in the elevator," Seth said slowly. "He whispered something I couldn't understand. Just one word. I guess he regained consciousness again in X ray. The doctor thinks he's asking for his sister, Roberta.''

"His sister? That doesn't seem all that unusual, does it?''

"The thing is,'' Seth said with obvious reluctance, "Wally and Roberta have never gotten along. When Shanna left home to come live out here at Wally's encouragement—'' He waved a hand through the air, unable to finish his thought. Because he couldn't talk about Shanna? Or was it just his concern for Wally?

"You're afraid Wally might be worse off than we think because he's asking for his sister,'' Levi guessed. "To make amends maybe before it's too late?''

Seth nodded. "It's the only reason I can think of that Wally would want to see his sister right now.''

"I'm sorry, Seth.'' Reaching for his hand, she gave it a quick squeeze. "He doesn't look like the kind of man who gives up easily.''

"No, just the opposite.''

"Did we do right not calling the police?''

"I just know what your father said about keeping the cops and FBI out of it,'' Seth said. "I think the paramedics and the doctor bought our story about him falling down the stairs and you trying to stop him and getting hit in the throat.''

Levi nodded. The man who'd attacked her wore thick gloves so there weren't any finger marks—yet. "In a few days we'll know who's behind all this and we can go to the police then.''

"Right.'' He didn't sound any more convinced than she was. "The doctor asked that we not stay too long. They'll be watching him closely but I've also asked a few friends of his to keep an eye on him. He should be safe.''

The clock on the wall read 1:45 a.m. as Levi followed Seth out of Wally's room, the door closing with a soft swish behind them, and down the hallway to the exit.

Outside, the night seemed more ominous, the clouds low, snow sifting down. The endless wind whipped the light snow, forming snow snakes that slithered across the pavement in dizzying designs. Tiny whirlwinds spun in the middle of the street and blew up to shower them with ice crystals.

Levi snuggled down in her coat, pulling her hat over her ears, her fingers flexing restlessly in her gloves.

"The problem is," Seth said as they stepped out into the night again, "Wally's the only one who knows who's after us."

"But hey, you're a trained professional and I'm...I'm going to want my own gun."

"Thanks for the vote of confidence."

"I have confidence in you," she said truthfully. "But who knows, you just might get yourself into trouble and need my help," she said, only half joking. "Seriously, Seth, even you have to admit my having a gun is a good idea."

"Yeah, terrific. It will make me feel a whole lot safer knowing you're armed." He frowned. "Carrying a gun can be a liability, Levi."

"Don't you think I've already heard all that," she said, and started to walk away from him.

He caught her arm. "I don't think you're ready to kill someone. Are you?"

"You think I'd let a killer take my gun away from me and use it on me?"

"No, not use it on you," Seth said. "I'm sure whoever is after us has his own gun. You'd probably have to make the decision whether to fire in a split second. If you don't fire, it could be your last mistake and a deadly one. These people are killers."

She met his gaze and saw real concern in his eyes and something she couldn't quite place. More regret? She swallowed hard, too aware of his hand still on her arm. His touch reminded her of earlier in the phone booth. "Okay. But I still want my own gun."

He groaned and released her.

"You might not always be there, Seth."

He let out a hoarse, low chuckle. "Can't argue that." Ahead, the wind sent a garbage can lid sailing across the street in front of them. As they passed, a trapped grocery bag blew to shreds in a chain-link fence. "I think we should find a place and get some rest."

She knew he was probably just suggesting it because of her. She didn't mind in the least. Exhaustion made her mind numb. Her body ached and her emotions rode too close to the surface; they felt more beat-up than her body.

It seemed darker, all the house lights extinguished, even the Christmas lights, as they walked down the residential street. The clouds still hung low but seemed darker, wetter, and the wind's howl more forlorn.

Levi couldn't help thinking about the man in the ski mask as they walked. It made her jumpy. She kept looking over her shoulder, waiting for him to leap out, cloaked by the darkness and snow, and the roar of the wind.

Seth seemed just as jumpy. For once, he slowed, shortening his strides to match hers as if he wanted to keep her as close as possible. He stopped at an all-night convenience store and bought them a couple of hot dogs. She thought she was too tired to eat, but the smell of the hot dogs proved her wrong. She wolfed it down, downing the meal with decaf coffee while Seth bought a hairbrush, shampoo, toothpaste and two toothbrushes.

"Thanks," she said, touched by his thoughtfulness as they left the store. She could see the Yellowstone River. The wind played at the surface of the water and tiny snowflakes touched down, melting into the dark depths.

A few blocks later he pointed at an older motel down near the river. "Let's see if we can stay there."

Levi saw a yoke-shaped neon sign hanging over the narrow entrance to the Old West Motel. Gateway To Yellowstone Park And The West, the smaller sign under it read. The U-shaped line of motel rooms looked weathered and worn and definitely western in their storefront design and rough wood exterior. Tall, ancient cottonwoods had grown around the place and, even without their leaves, seemed to shelter the rooms, providing cover.

"Looks great," she said, not caring where they stayed. Any place out of the wind and snow and cold sounded great right now. Her body begged for sleep, but she wondered if she would be able to close her eyes knowing there was a killer after them.

"I'll see if I can get us a room," Seth said beside her.

She could smell the river as Seth pushed the bell. A buzzer sounded and a few moments later, the motel office door opened. She didn't pay much attention as Seth registered. The woman behind the counter squinted over the smoke from the cigarette dangling in her thin, red lips, but she seemed more interested in the cash Seth laid on the counter than them.

Levi let her attention wander to the window. She couldn't get it out of her head that she and this cowboy were on the run together—she didn't even know who they were running from or when she'd get to go home again. If ever.

Wally was the only one with answers—and he was unconscious and possibly dying. And she'd come face-to-face with at least one of the people after her. She knew she'd never be able to forget his eyes until she unmasked him—and kept him from ever coming after her again.

And then there was Seth. Although he tried hard to keep it a secret from her, she could see that he had ghosts from his past to deal with. That worried her, making this whole thing feel all the more dangerous. She didn't kid herself. As capable and independent as she was, she was no match for killers. Her life was in Seth Gantry's hands.

Levi jumped when Seth touched her elbow. "Just tired," she whispered, as he led her outside into the windstorm and down the cracked concrete walk to Room Seven. Lucky seven, right?

He inserted the key, swung open the door and reached in to turn on the lights.

She blinked and stared at the room, then at the man beside her. Just what had she gotten herself into anyway?

SETH WASN'T TOO SURPRISED to see that the room was small, smelled like a basement and was distinctly green. Green in a variety of shades from the chartreuse chenille bedspread to the variegated shag rug. The walls were dark knotty-pine paneling, framing the bed like a box.

'It's…quaint, huh?'' he said, and looked over at Levi.

"Cozy," she said, sounding nervous. Not that he could blame her. It had been that kind of day.

He felt a little nervous himself. After spending hours in the cab of an old pickup with this woman, what was so different about a small green motel room?

The bed, fool. It dwarfed the room. The only space between it and the walls was the worn traffic pattern in the rug on three sides. One of those paths broke off to lead to a tiny green room off to the right. He could make out a toilet and a shower stall.

Well, he hadn't brought her here to impress her or seduce her, he thought. As if he could do either. "I think we should get some sleep," he said as he ushered her into the room and closed the door.

He watched her look around for a place to sit and realized the bed was it. Or the toilet.

He sat on the edge of the bed. It groaned under his weight, making her look over at him.

He smiled. They were acting like newlyweds. ''Come on,'' he said, patting the space beside him.

"You're safe for the rest of tonight, princess. I promise."

He shrugged out of his coat, pulled the pistol from the pocket and slid it under his pillow. Then he pulled off his boots and lay back on his elbows.

"Bed's not so bad," he commented. "Turn out the light and come lie down."

She stood for a moment, her look saying she would rather be anywhere than here with him. He could understand that.

She turned out the light. Only a little illumination came through the curtains of the small window. Just enough that he could see her as she lay down beside him.

The wind had finally stopped, leaving behind an eerie stillness. In the light through the curtain, he could see that it was snowing harder. Large, lacy flakes.

"Would you hold me?"

He thought he'd heard wrong. "What?" he asked softly, looking over at her. He could see a tear, like a tiny diamond, at the corner of her left eye.

"Would you just—"

He pulled her to him and wrapped his arms around her. She buried her face in his chest, her breath warm and moist through his shirt. He could feel her heart, a beating drum. He wanted to tell her that everything was going to be all right, but he couldn't lie to her. Instead, he prayed he could keep her safe. For tonight he had the pistol and Levi in his arms.

With any other woman, he'd have been thinking he might get lucky. But not with this one. He felt lucky just lying next to her, holding her, knowing how hard it must have been for her, as tough and independent as she was, to ask him.

When she glanced up at him, he looked into the deep violet of her eyes. It took everything in him not to kiss her again. But he knew if he did, he'd be lost. He'd never kissed any woman who made him feel like Levi did. Not in years. Eight to be exact.

He pulled her closer until her head rested on his chest. After a few moments, she relaxed. He lay motionless, not even breathing for a few seconds, trying to understand the wave of emotion she evoked in him.

She wasn't like anyone he'd ever known. Levi was different. She made him feel different. With her, he was having trouble keeping up the emotional barricade he'd built after Shanna.

He let himself go, believing just for tonight that he could love again. That the ghosts of his past could no longer haunt him. For just tonight, he was merely a man, holding a very special woman, a woman who could love a man like him.

He knew how dangerous thinking like that was as he buried his face in her hair, breathing in the sweet, clean scent of her, and closed his eyes.

Chapter Nine

Friday, November 26, 1999

Levi awoke to the howling of the wind. She blinked, trying to place where she was. Not in her room at the ranch. Not anywhere she could recall. But then it was so dark and warm, like being in a cocoon. That cocoon feeling, she realized, was enhanced by the warm body lying next to her and the long, muscular arm wrapped around her. She rolled over onto her back, the arm coming to lie across her breasts as she stared at the man beside her.

Everything came back in an instant at just the sight of Seth Gantry. She reminded herself that she still didn't know a lot about the cowboy. Next to nothing, in fact. But that didn't keep her from feeling warm and protected waking in his arms. Sleep had softened his strong features, making him even more handsome and not quite so...intense.

She felt him stir and suddenly she didn't want to be lying there when he woke up.

Carefully she slid out of his arms and off the bed. She stood for a moment staring down at him, then she headed for the shower and the only privacy the motel room afforded.

She locked herself in the tiny cubicle, feeling strangely vulnerable, considering the man in the next room was her protector.

Once in the shower, she lost track of time, just letting the hot water flow over her: this might be her last shower. Bad thought, she admonished herself.

She might have stayed in there longer but unfortunately, the water eventually turned cold. She took her time drying off, tied the towel around her and brushed her teeth, then her hair, wondering if Seth was awake yet.

She was just starting to reach for her clothes when she heard him cry out.

At least she thought it was Seth.

"Seth?" she inquired cautiously, stepping up to the door to listen. Was that a moan she heard?

Her mind raced. The killer had found them and attacked Seth!

With a groan she quickly searched the bathroom and just as quickly saw that there wasn't anything she could use for a weapon. Realizing she was still naked, she quickly pulled on the jeans and scrambled into the shirt, buttoning only a couple of buttons. Cautiously, she opened the bathroom door a crack and peeked out.

Seth lay sprawled on the bed alone, his eyes still closed. There didn't appear to be anyone else in the room. She opened the bathroom door a little wider and stuck her head out. The chain was still on the outside door and no one was in the room other than her and Seth.

Frowning, she stepped closer to the bed, thinking

the sound must have come from the next room. "No," Seth cried, his face twisted in pain, his brow beaded with sweat. He squirmed on the bed, whispering, "No, no, oh, God, no."

With relief she saw that he was just having a bad dream.

She stepped closer, trying to remember what she'd heard about waking a person from a dream. Touching his shoulder, she gently shook him, not wanting to scare him. "Seth?"

"Nooo!" He bolted upright in the bed and grabbed her.

She tried to step back but he was too fast and too strong. He seized her, dragging her down onto the bed with him. His arms wrapped around her in a fierce hug and his mouth found hers, as unerring as sonar. The kiss was passionate and possessive and, it appeared, just a preview.

She sucked in a breath as his lips left hers to drop kisses down her neck. Suddenly his face burrowed into her open shirt, loosening the buttons, until his mouth found the bare skin of her shoulder, his mustache tickling her in a way that was definitely not funny.

Levi froze, unsure what to do. "Uh, Seth?"

"Oh, Shanna," he whispered.

Shanna? The girl in the photograph at Wally's. Wally's niece. She'd seen Seth's reaction to the photo. Hadn't she suspected Shanna was the woman who'd broken his heart? Now it seemed pretty certain that was the case.

Worse yet, he thought *she* was Shanna.

His lips began a heated trail along her bare skin from her shoulder downward toward the rise of her breast. She felt her body react of its own volition to the combination of warmth, wetness and the soft, silky, sensual brush of his mustache.

"Seth?" she said in earnest, not sure of the fastest way to get him back to waking reality, but anxious to get him there. *"Seth,"* she said more forcefully, as forcefully as she could with her sore throat, accompanied by a swift smack of her hand on his shoulder. Waking him abruptly might be risky for him, but letting him continue was downright dangerous for her.

His mouth reached the peak of her breast. He sucked the pebble-hard nipple into his mouth.

"Seth!" It came out a strangled plea, although at that point she wasn't sure what she was pleading for.

His tongue slowed its glorious caresses, his mouth released her. She felt his arms loosen from around her, and his lips rose slowly from her heated, moist flesh.

She pulled back about the same time he did. He blinked. She crawled off the bed to stand, quickly straightening her shirt, covering the bare parts he'd exposed to his kisses.

He pushed off the opposite side of the bed to stand. He looked disoriented, as if he'd never seen her before and, at the same time, she noticed with a furtive glance, aroused.

"It's all right," she said, embarrassed for both of them. "You just had a bad dream."

He nodded and looked around the motel room, still appearing confused as to where he was, whom he was with. She watched him drag himself out of

the nightmare and finally focus on her. Obviously
he'd expected Shanna. Wanted Shanna.

"A bad dream?" he asked softly.

Levi nodded, her body refusing to forget the feel
of his mouth, the heat of his breath against her bare
skin. She shivered and crossed her arms over her
breasts, more aware than ever that she wasn't wearing a bra and the fact that he'd aroused her—something she noticed he had noticed.

He smiled and raised his gaze back up to hers.
"Levi." He sounded surprised.

"You just had a bad dream," Levi repeated as
she stepped back, trying to put some distance between them, only to bang into the wall. The man
must think her an incredible klutz, first after that kiss
in the phone booth and now this.

"I'd just gotten out of the shower when I…heard
you…calling out," she tried to explain. Why did she
feel the need to explain? She hadn't started this.

He nodded, still eyeing her across the expanse of
the mattress. "I think I'll take a shower," he said,
his voice deep and a little rough. He stepped into
the bathroom and closed the door. Almost immediately, she heard the sound of water running.

She stood looking after him for a moment, then
sat down on the edge of the bed, groaning inwardly
when it moaned under her weight. Geez, what had
that been all about? As if she didn't know. Shanna.
Had he also wished he'd been kissing Shanna last
night in the phone booth? Who was this woman anyway? And what had she done to Seth?

One thing was for sure. Levi needed to keep her
distance from this heartsick cowboy. Not easy in the
situation she was in. Even harder since whatever

haunted Seth made her all the more intrigued by him and his secret past. Intrigued and attracted.

SETH DIDN'T TAKE a long shower. Probably, Levi remembered belatedly, because she'd used all the hot water.

The phone rang, startling her but not half as much as when Seth burst from the bathroom clad only in jeans, his hair wet and slicked back, his jaw cleanly shaved, the mustache still thick and dark curling over his lip.

"Don't answer that," he ordered.

It rang again and they both stared at it.

"No one knows where we are, do they?" she asked in a hushed whisper.

Seth shook his head. Water drops clung to his eyelashes, making his eyes dark, inviting pools. He held a towel in one hand, indicating he'd started to dry his hair before he came out of the bathroom at a run.

He seemed a little flustered, something new, she thought. Could it be because of the incident on the bed this morning? Was it possible that at some point it hadn't all been about Shanna?

Yeah, right. Levi knew she just wanted to believe that because it made her feel a little better. It was hard enough for her to admit how much she'd enjoyed his advances without thinking they'd been intended for another woman.

"If no one knows we're here, then it must be the motel office," she said reasonably as the phone rang again.

He stared at her for a moment, then shrugged

sheepishly and, in two easy strides, picked up the phone. "Hello?"

She studied his muscular arms and chest, transfixed. A dusting of tightly curled dark hair trailed tantalizingly down, tapering into a thin line to disappear into his jeans. The man stirred something in her that had never been stirred quite like this before.

She watched him frown as he listened to whoever was on the other end of the line. "Yes. Thank you." He hung up the phone and looked up at her. "The office. The rental car I ordered last night has been delivered."

She nodded and grinned. "A little paranoia is good."

He returned her grin, his gaze meeting hers. It only lasted an instant, the spark that leaped between them, but it ignited something inside her that sent a flush of heat racing through her.

Don't do this to me, Seth.

He dropped his gaze, appearing to have heard her silent plea. Then as if suddenly realizing he was only half-dressed, he rushed back into the bathroom to emerge again, only moments later, fully dressed. But it didn't make any difference. Some men had all-male sex appeal, Levi thought. Seth Gantry had it in spades. Just her luck, being on the run with him, of all cowboys. A cowboy with an old girlfriend named Shanna and a whole lot of heartache. Yep, just her luck.

"About earlier..." he began.

She groaned inwardly, knowing this time he was definitely going to apologize. She swore she'd kick him if he did.

"I'm not exactly sure what happened this morning in my dream, but—'' He grinned. ''I really liked the part right before I woke up.''

She felt herself flush. Yeah, well, too bad it had been another woman's name on his lips. She busied herself by picking up their few belongings, all the while admonishing herself for getting so close to this cowboy. The man was walking heartbreak. Any fool could see that.

Seth called the hospital before they left the motel room. Wally was still unconscious but stable.

She watched Seth pull on his coat, wishing they didn't have to leave this awful motel. She'd felt safe for a while here.

''I thought we'd go back to Wally's office first and see what we can find in that mess.'' He studied her openly as he settled his Stetson on his dark head. ''If you'd prefer not to, you can stay here. I'll leave you the pistol. Lock the door behind me.''

She shook her head as she reached for her coat. ''You may need the pistol and you might need my help.''

OH, HE NEEDED HELP all right, Seth thought as they left the motel. The cold shower he'd taken hadn't helped much. She'd said he'd had a bad dream. He wished he could remember it. But how bad could a dream be if you woke up with a beautiful, half-naked sensuous woman in your arms?

He'd certainly been surprised. But she'd seemed just as surprised. As much as he wondered about the dream, he wasn't about to ask. But he couldn't quit thinking about the ending of it. Or Levi. Or her physical response. Both stirred long-dormant desire in him. Just what he needed, as if he and Levi weren't in enough trouble.

It was almost ten in the morning. Seth couldn't believe he'd slept so late. He knew it was because he'd fallen asleep with—and woken up to—Levi in his arms.

He had to admit that everything that had happened Thanksgiving Day seemed unreal in the light of day. Especially this beautiful day. The sun shone high overhead and the sky was clear and blue. A Chinook had blown in instead of a snowstorm. The wind was now downright warm; the snow that had fallen last night had either blown away or melted off. The weather felt almost balmy. Almost like Texas.

But Levi's hoarse voice and the bruises on her neck where she'd been attacked last night were chilling reminders of how far from Texas they really were, making nothing about the day seem innocuous. Wally was still in the hospital, unconscious, the bad guys would know by now that he and Levi definitely weren't in the ashes of Wally's cabin and someone would be coming after them to finish the job. Seth had to find out why and stop them.

As he and Levi walked toward the black four-wheel-drive Blazer parked at the curb, he breathed in the mountain air, filling himself with the scents and smells of Montana, unconsciously refueling. This place had always had a settling effect on him, he thought, trying to concentrate his thoughts on anything but the woman beside him.

"As bad as this all has been, it's nice to be back, huh," Levi said quietly.

He glanced over at her, telling himself there was no way she could understand. She was just fishing.

"I used to feel that way about the ranch when I came home from college," she said, looking toward the mountains. "I would just breathe it in as if I couldn't get enough before I had to leave again."

"Yeah." He studied her with surprise and acknowledged the ache inside him. For the past eight years he'd believed that ache was only Shanna. Shanna and Montana had been one. Was it possible he could separate the two at last?

"I've missed this," he admitted as he opened Levi's side of the car.

"I can tell," she said as she climbed in. But she didn't push. Didn't even look at him as he started the car. It wasn't like her, he thought. What was up?

He drove to Wally's office building in more traffic than he could remember in Livingston. The weather had brought people out. That and the fact that today was the busiest shopping day of the year.

He parked behind Wally's van and climbed out, wondering if there was anything in that ransacked office that would help them or if they were just wasting their time. It seemed a long shot at best since the attacker had already gone through everything. But they had nothing else.

Levi followed him up the steps. The front door was still locked. He felt the pistol in his coat pocket as he led Levi around back again. He wondered if she wouldn't have been safer at the motel. The problem was, he didn't want to let her out of his sight and he didn't think anyone would strike in broad daylight, not today, as busy as the streets were.

This time the back door was locked, as well, but

he'd gotten the key from Wally's personal effects at the hospital.

He shot Levi a look, expecting some smart comment. She'd been too quiet. Was it her throat bothering her? Or coming back here after what had happened last night?

When his gaze met hers, he felt the same pull he had earlier.

Levi pulled her gaze away first, leaving him wondering if he'd done something to upset her. Who was he kidding? He'd done little else.

He shook off the sharp stab of desire he felt for her. He hadn't felt this kind of desire, desire that was more than simply physical, for a woman since—since Shanna. So why was he feeling it now? Because Levi reminded him of Shanna? The funny thing was, he thought as he pushed open the door and pulled Levi in after him, it was becoming harder and harder to see any resemblance between the two women.

Inside the building, their footfalls echoed softly down the linoleum-tiled hallway. He motioned for Levi to be as quiet as possible, not that she'd made a sound. He suspected she was already holding her breath, expecting every shadow to jump out at them, just as he was.

But the building didn't seem so ominous in the daylight. Just too quiet. Too empty, he thought.

Pushing open the door to the stairs, he climbed quickly to the third-floor landing, wishing he hadn't had to see Wally's destroyed wheelchair again. It lay on its side, reminding him that his friend might be dying.

Seth had locked both doors of Wally's office before the paramedics had arrived. He used the key now to unlock the hall door.

"Where should we begin?" Levi asked as she stepped gingerly in behind him.

He heard the slight quiver in her tough-girl tone and saw her glance toward the closet. The door stood open, the closet empty. He went to the closet door and closed it, then closed and locked the door they'd come in through, as well.

Levi smiled her thanks to him and knelt down to pick up a file. "Do you have any idea what we're looking for?"

He shook his head as he turned on the overhead light. "I'm just hoping I know when I see it. We probably won't find anything that makes any sense but we have to try. It's all we have."

She nodded and put the file folder she'd retrieved from the floor on the bare desktop. "Why don't I stack the files on his desk so you can go through them?"

"Sounds like a good idea." He pulled up a chair and sat down. "How's your throat?"

"Fine."

"It isn't bothering you?" he asked.

She turned to look at him. "Why would you think something was bothering me?"

Well, that cinched it. He was smart enough to know that when a woman said that, something was definitely bothering her. But he didn't push it.

Nor did she, thankfully. "Wally must be incredibly organized," she said as she handed him a stack of files.

"What gave you that idea in all this mess?" he

asked, surprised that she'd figured that out about Wally.

"All the files are neatly labeled, color-coded and alphabetized," she answered. "Surprisingly, they don't seem to be that mixed up."

Seth watched Levi chew at her cheek as she glanced around the room, then knelt down to pick up a well-used scratch pad from the floor. She put it down on the desk and retrieved a pencil from the floor. He could see that the top sheet of the pad was blank but had indentations where something had been written on the sheet above it.

As she tried the old trick of scribbling lightly across the blank sheet with a pencil, he chuckled to himself, then went back to sorting through the files she'd given him. He didn't hold much stock in her amateur sleuthing, but he had to give her credit for trying.

"Anything?" he asked, grinning at her.

She held it up. Unfortunately, the scratch pad netted nothing more than a bunch of what looked like doodles and two words, written in large block letters and circled. Robson's Cleaners.

"Wally had made himself a note to go to the cleaners," she said, tossing the scratch pad down. "Terrific."

She went back to work picking up file folders, but he could tell she was deep in thought. Her eyes turned a dark violet, her brows furrowed and she caught her lower lip in her teeth again as she scooped up a single file folder and stopped. He watched her open it and suck in her breath.

"What?" he asked.

She looked up at him as if surprised that he'd

been watching her. More and more he had trouble keeping his eyes off her.

"Just a theory," she said.

"Let's hear it." He leaned back in the chair to give her his undivided attention.

"Whoever did this didn't bother to dump the contents out of most of the file folders," she said. "I think he knew what he was looking for. Maybe something that would incriminate him?"

"That seems logical," he agreed.

She smiled, appeared encouraged and continued. "Here's my theory," she said with more enthusiasm. "Whoever attacked Wally, knew him, knew how well-organized he was. My guess is that the attacker checked the filing cabinet. When he didn't find a file under his name, he got frustrated and didn't know where to look so he just started throwing things."

Seth raised a brow.

"What makes you think the guy didn't find what he was looking for?"

"He was so busy tearing up this office that he didn't even notice Wally had crawled to the elevator."

"Good point." How had he forgotten how sharp this woman was?

"What if Wally *hadn't* filed it yet?" she said excitedly. "At the ranch, I always keep a couple of working folders handy until I'm through with the business inside, then I file the papers."

"What exactly do you do at the ranch?" he asked, curious.

She shot him a look. "I know you think I'm just

a spoiled rich girl, but I've been running the ranch for two years now."

He *was* surprised.

She smiled as if she liked surprising him.

"Please continue," he said gallantly.

She crossed her arms over the single file folder pressed to her chest. "Wally color-coded his files. See." She nodded to a stack on the desk. "Those are all either blue, green or yellow."

"What do the different colors mean?"

She shrugged. "I have no idea. However," she added quickly, "what if what the killer was looking for was in Wally's working folder?"

"That's one hell of a leap," Seth said, but waited expectantly to see what she'd come up with. He had a feeling she might be on to something.

"It is a leap, I admit." Levi chewed at her lower lip for a moment, unwittingly drawing his gaze to her mouth. She stopped gnawing at her lip. The office shrank and the thermostat peaked. She uncrossed her arms and laid the file folder on the desk.

"This is the only one I've found that has a red label," she said softly. "Also everything in it seems recent and random, you know what I mean?"

It took a moment for his gaze to shift to the folder. "I think I do."

SETH STARED AT THE FOLDER on the desk for a moment, too aware of the woman across that expanse of wood. The air seemed to pulse between them. He took a breath and reached for the file, expecting it to be warm to his touch after the way she'd held it to her breasts.

He opened it. Unless he wanted to get them both

killed, he had to get his mind on business. He settled his gaze on the papers in the folder, at first seeing nothing but her lips, thinking of nothing but the feel of them on his. Remembering this morning and the feel of her breasts.

Then the papers came into focus and he sat up a little straighter.

Damned if he didn't think she was right and that this was Wally's working folder.

"The papers probably won't be in order since they'd been spilled," she warned him. "But I think they're all there. I was careful to pick up everything nearby."

Seth thumbed through the file. Several divorce cases. A child custody dispute. A possible wandering wife. A missing person. A skip trace. Several requests for background checks.

He continued to leaf through the papers, feeling more frustrated as he neared the end of the stack. How was he ever going to figure out if one of these was related to the murder plot against Levi?

He hadn't been paying any attention to what Levi was doing until he heard the click of the answering machine. He looked up when the messages began to play, then back to the papers in front of him when the first several messages proved to be nothing of interest.

His breath caught in his throat as he looked down at the last paper in the folder. A letter from the Department of Corrections, Montana State Prison Department in Deer Lodge. His fingers shook and he had to place the sheet of paper on the desk to read it.

"What is it?" he heard Levi ask in concern.

He couldn't answer. He stared at the paper in front of him, his heart pounding. "'Because of your interest in this case and your personal involvement, we wish to inform you that Alex Wells has been released on parole.'" The letter was dated more than two weeks ago.

Just then the answering machine clicked to the next message and the voice that filled the office made Seth's head jerk up. His mouth turned to dust as he heard the familiar voice.

"Wally? Dammit, Wally, pick up. It's Alex." Then the machine clicked off, filling the office with leaden silence.

Alex's voice brought it all back. Their friendship. Shanna. The death of both the friendship and Shanna. Seth stumbled to his feet, knocking a stack of file folders onto the floor.

"Who is Alex Wells?" Levi demanded, taking the letter from him.

He stared at her, his vision blurred by his shock. By his fury. "The man who killed Shanna."

Chapter Ten

"Killed Shanna?" Levi repeated in disbelief.

Seth had gone deathly white and appeared to be fighting for each breath. He stood with his hands on top of the desk for support, his mouth a tight line, his eyes dark and filled with pain. When he finally spoke, his voice raw with anguish, his words fell as hard and heavy as stones. "Alex murdered her eight years ago. Now it seems he's out of prison. And, no doubt, out after me."

"What do you mean, after *you?*" she asked, trying to make sense of what he was saying. "You don't think he's the one we're running from?"

Seth didn't answer.

Levi stared at him. She'd just assumed Shanna had broken Seth's heart and that was the source of his pain. But now she realized it was much more than that. "Seth, what's going on?"

He shook his head. "It's a long story."

"Then give me the abbreviated version."

He studied her for a lengthy moment. "Not here," he said finally, and headed for the door.

Levi followed, in shock. Shanna dead. Murdered. Another piece of the Seth puzzle. But she knew the main pieces were still missing. And she wasn't sure which ones she wanted most. The one that explained why Seth thought this killer was now after them? Or the one that told her just what Shanna had meant to him?

As Levi passed the spilled file cabinet, she glanced down. A name on one of the folders caught her eye. She scooped it up off the floor and followed Seth out.

Seth drove them away from Wally's office and out of town, headed south. Levi saw a sign. Yellowstone Park 52 Miles. In the distance, she could see where the mountains opened in rocky bluffs and river bottom. Another valley, this one larger and longer, opened just beyond.

"Where are we going?" she asked, afraid his latest plan was to run from his past again, just as he'd no doubt done eight years ago when he'd ended up in Texas. She was afraid where they'd end up this time. But more than anything, she was afraid to hear what he had to tell her. "Mexico is nice this time of year."

He glanced over at her then, some of the color coming back into his face. "I thought we'd go someplace a little closer. Carter's Bridge."

"Are we planning to jump?"

"Maybe," he said, and turned onto East River Road. Just past the bridge, he turned into a fishing access site. It was empty of other vehicles. Seth parked and got out. She followed him down to the river's edge, knowing he was finally going to tell her about Shanna, about his past and what had made him leave Montana eight years ago. Isn't that what she'd wanted? Suddenly she wasn't so sure.

She realized she liked Seth. Actually, had grown rather fond of him over the past seventeen hours—all physical attraction and reaction aside.

When Seth sat down on the lee side of a large boulder, she sat next to him and looked out at the water. The wind rippled the dark green surface and stirred the leafless limbs of the cottonwoods. A large white cloud drifted through the endless blue overhead.

"I know you were in love with her," she said, unable to stand it any longer.

"What makes you say that?" he asked, glancing over at her in obvious surprise.

She didn't tell him she'd guessed the moment she'd seen the pain in his eyes. "You were calling out her name in your sleep."

"Ah." He nodded. "So that's why you were looking at me as though I had two heads this morning. Probably also explains why you've been so quiet. Must have made you wonder about me, me calling out another woman's name as I was getting…acquainted with you."

He shook his head at her as if she should have told him and he'd have cleared the whole thing up. Right. The way he wasn't clearing it up right now?

"I figured you were asleep," she said. "I didn't think anything of it."

"You didn't, huh?" He smiled at her for a moment and she would have sworn he was remembering her obvious reaction poking against her braless shirt.

She felt herself flush, the day suddenly seeming much hotter. "You were going to tell me about Shanna."

His gaze cast out over the water, his features hardened. "The short version? Shanna and I dated for a little over a year. Then she fell in love with my best friend. Alex had always had a way with women. He swept her off her feet. I thought he was all wrong for her, but I wasn't about to stand in her way. Alex seemed to make her happy, so I gave her my blessing. And he killed her."

Levi stared at Seth. "Why did he kill her?"

Seth shook his head. "No one but Alex knows that. He swears he didn't do it. He swears he loved her."

"But there must have been some reason he was convicted for her murder?"

Seth nodded. "The night she died, Shanna had found out there was at least one other woman in Alex's life. Shanna was determined to confront him. I tried to convince her to wait until morning, but she wouldn't listen. She drove out to Alex's place. It was the last time I saw her alive."

Levi felt sick inside.

"Wally and I found her in the railroad car Alex had converted into a house on the edge of town," Seth continued. "She'd been shot in the heart at point-blank range. We found Alex in one of the abandoned railroad buildings near the river."

"What was he doing there?" Levi asked.

"He said he'd chased the killer there. The old railroad roundhouse was once used to work on locomotives. Wally fell from one of the walkways trying to stop Alex. The cops never found any evidence there was another person in the building besides Alex."

"That's what put Wally in the wheelchair, the

fall,'' she said, and Seth nodded. Wally wasn't the only one scarred for life by what had happened, she thought. ''You believe Alex killed her.''

He said nothing as he got up and went to stand next to the edge of the river, his back to her. ''I think they argued. He'd been drinking with some friends at a local bar just before that. I think he shot her, then came up with the story of the fleeing killer to try to save his neck. Shanna was shot with the same gun found on Alex when he was arrested at the roundhouse. Alex said he'd picked up the gun from the crime scene to chase the killer who he'd heard getting away. He was found guilty of second-degree murder.''

''I'm so sorry, Seth.'' She stared at his broad back. ''But why would he mean you any harm?''

Seth came back over to her. ''Alex says he was framed for Shanna's murder.'' Seth offered her a hand up. She took it and let him pull her to her feet. ''He thinks I framed him. He swore he'd come after me when he got out. I think he has.''

''He thinks *you* killed Shanna?'' she cried. ''Why?''

Seth shook his head. ''Jealousy, I guess. That if I couldn't have her, I couldn't stand anyone else having her. Especially him.''

She stared at Seth.

He nodded and shrugged. ''You aren't sure either, huh?''

''No,'' she said quickly. ''You're not a killer, Seth. I'd stake my life on it.''

''You *are* staking your life on it, Levi. I wouldn't blame you if you wanted to call your father and ask him to find someone else to protect you.''

She shook her head. Her gaze settled on his. "You got me into his, Gantry, and damned if you aren't going to have to see it through."

He studied her for a long moment, his eyes locked with hers. "Suit yourself," he said finally.

"I will."

As SETH DROVE THEM BACK into town, he felt warmed by Levi's faith in him. He told himself that the woman didn't know him. Her faith was misplaced. But still it made him feel better about what he had to do.

What he couldn't get over was that Alex was already out of prison. Probably for good behavior. Where was Alex right now? Out there watching them? Seth couldn't shake off the feeling that someone had been watching them.

"He doesn't look...dangerous," Levi said, frowning down at what he saw was a folder lying open in her lap.

"Where did you get that?" he asked, seeing Alex's blond, blue-eyed, boy-next-door face looking up at Levi.

"I found it in Wally's office," she said. "I don't think this was what the attacker had been looking for. It was too easy to find."

Seth thought about that for a moment. Then what had the attacker wanted?

"He certainly doesn't look like a murderer," Levi said.

No, nothing about Alex looked like a killer. But then who knew what made a man take another person's life? Seth had known Alex Wells for most of his life. Alex was the last man Seth would suspect could do such a thing. Especially to a woman Alex had sworn he loved. Look how wrong Seth had been.

"Believe me, he's dangerous," Seth told Levi. "Don't let his looks fool you."

"Seth, how can you be so sure he's the one after us?" she asked, closing the folder. "This all began because Wally found out about some murder plot against me, right? Alex doesn't even know me. Also, it's been eight years. Maybe he's put the past behind him. Maybe he just wants to get on with his life."

"You don't know Alex."

She shook her head. "Why would Wally involve you in this if Alex was behind it? Wouldn't Wally be worried about getting you killed?"

Seth had asked himself the same thing. Wally had certainly known about the animosity between Seth and Alex. Judging by the date on the letter from the prison, Wally had known for more than two weeks that Alex was getting out on parole. Why hadn't Wally warned Seth? And why had Alex called Wally? What had he wanted? "Obviously Alex hasn't forgotten or he wouldn't have called Wally sounding so upset. We won't know until Wally regains consciousness. Or we find Alex."

"Find Alex?" she echoed.

He could feel her gaze on him. Not the soft, sweet silk of pale lavender, but the dark violet, no-nonsense, tough-ranch-woman glare.

"Seth, from the photo in the folder, Alex's eyes are blue. The man who attacked me last night in Wally's office had gray eyes."

"I know that man wasn't Alex, Levi. Alex is leaner and taller."

"Then shouldn't we be looking for the man who attacked Wally?" she asked.

"We find Alex and we'll find the man," he said with conviction.

"Seth, how can you be so sure?"

He doubted she'd appreciate hearing about his gut instinct. Nor did he think she'd want to hear that he suspected her resemblance to Shanna had played a part in this somehow. The truth was, he had no idea how Levi had become involved. He just knew Alex was in on it somehow. Just as he knew she wasn't going to like his answer.

"I don't know how or why or what it could possibly have to do with you or your father," he admitted finally. "But yes, Levi, Alex is involved in this. I feel it."

"Well, at least you have good reason to believe it's Alex." She shook her head in obvious frustration. "Seth, what if you're wrong? What if you're so busy running from Alex that you don't recognize the real killer after us?"

The thought had crossed his mind, he had to admit. But he didn't think admitting it to Levi would be a good idea. Especially right now.

"Maybe you're too close to this and it's throwing off your instincts," she continued quickly. "Don't get me wrong, I'm a big fan of your gut instincts. They saved our lives back at the cabin, but a little common sense would be nice, too. Why would Alex want to kill *me?*"

Because at first glance Levi looked so much like

Shanna? He parked across the street from Martin's Café. "I'm hungry, how about you?"

"You're kidding, right?" she asked, looking around. "You want to have breakfast now? After you just told me that this Alex person is after us? Shouldn't we get out of town and hide somewhere?"

Seth shook his head. "What good would it do? If I'm right, he'd only track us down and kill us."

"Then let's hope you're wrong."

"Then someone else will only track us down and try to kill us," he said, opening his car door. "Either way, we have a killer after us. Running isn't going to help." He got out and locked the door behind him.

As he started across the street toward the café, he heard her car door fly open, then slam behind her.

"What *is* going to help?" she demanded, catching up to him. When he didn't answer, she asked, "Are you telling me you have a plan?"

"Maybe." He glanced at her.

She mugged a face at him. "Sure you do."

He held the door for her as they entered Martin's, an old-time railroad café that was still connected by a covered walkway to the former depot-turned-museum. His gaze was on the regulars who'd gathered rather than the old-time-café look of the place, from the worn vinyl booths to the faded Formica tabletops. A local landmark and meeting spot, the café was nearly packed.

Levi slid into a booth that had just emptied out and Seth sat across from her where he could see the doorway and the street. He glanced around the café as the waitress appeared, her hands full. He spotted some ranchers he knew at the back, but didn't see who he was looking for.

"Teresa working today?" he asked as the waitress dropped a couple of plastic-covered menus onto the table, then put down two empty cups, balancing a full pot of coffee in the other hand.

"She's in the kitchen. Coffee?"

He and Levi both nodded and the waitress filled their cups. "I'll tell Teresa you're here and give you a minute to look at the menu," she said before taking off to empty the pot at the next table.

"Who's Teresa?" Levi asked.

"An old friend," he said simply, and took a sip of the hot coffee, letting it take away some of the chill he'd felt ever since he'd heard Alex had been released from prison. He watched Levi tear the lid from one of the creamers and pour it into her coffee, telling himself she was probably right. He *was* too close to this. Maybe Alex wasn't after them. Maybe it was someone else, someone who'd have a better motive for wanting a senator's daughter dead.

Was he just chasing his own ghosts? Worse yet, was he taking Levi along, endangering her even more by involving her in his past?

The problem was, Alex was his only lead. And his gut instinct told him Alex was the key. It was too much of a coincidence that someone had tried to kill him and Levi *and* Wally, and Alex had just been released from prison.

But Seth knew it didn't really make any difference why he was going after Alex. He was. And he wouldn't know if Alex was involved until he found him—or Alex found them. Seth knew it was just a matter of time till he'd be seeing his old friend again.

When the waitress returned, Seth noticed that Levi hadn't even opened her menu. "Two breakfast specials?" he suggested.

She nodded, seemingly more interested in the people in the café. "Do you think this is safe?" she asked as she turned to look behind her. The door opened and, on a gust of wind, two ranchers blew in. They stomped their feet on the mat by the door, then went to sit at the counter.

Seth glanced toward the bank of windows that faced Park Street. Cars and pickups drove by; on the sidewalk, a woman carried a stack of brightly wrapped Christmas packages to her car.

Everything looked so normal, so ordinary. Sitting here in the warmth of the café, the familiar smells of coffee and bacon and pancakes wafting out of the kitchen, listening to the rattle of dishes and the discussion of cattle prices and weather patterns, who would have thought they were in danger?

"This place seems so out in the open." Levi shivered, and took a sip of her coffee.

Their eyes met over the top of her cup.

"Oh, my God," she whispered as she put the cup down with a thunk. "You did this on purpose. You want him to know."

"If Alex doesn't know we're looking for him, he will by the end of the day."

She stared at him. "Are you nuts?"

"Trust me, Levi, if we don't find him, he'll find us. I like to know what I'm walking into."

"Excuse me, but it sounds like *we're* walking into a trap."

He couldn't really argue that point. "It's complicated," he said, and looked toward the street. "My philosophy is that some things you just can't plan for. You have to wait and see." He swung his gaze back to her. "Like meeting you."

"Seth—"

The waitress appeared and slid plates in front of each of them. Levi looked startled as the table began to shake and the coffee sloshed in the cups.

"The train tracks are right outside," the waitress said, and laughed at Levi's alarmed expression. A whistle blew and kept blowing as the train neared. The noise grew louder and louder until it filled the café.

The train rumbled by, muting all but the sound of the whistle and the clatter of wheels on the track just outside the door.

"You're not from Livingston, are you?" the waitress said over the roar as she refilled their coffee cups. "More than twenty trains come through this town in a day, whistles blowing. Used to be over thirty a day."

Seth had forgotten the trains. He liked the sound of them and realized it was just another thing he'd missed.

"You should hear them on New Year's Eve," the waitress was saying. "The engineer blows the whistle all the way through town." She looked at Seth. "Teresa will be right out."

Levi stared wide-eyed at him until the train and the noise finally died off in the distance. Surprisingly, she seemed at a loss for words. He wasn't sure if it was the train or what he'd said to her before.

After a moment, her gaze shifted to the plate in front of her. It was filled with chicken-fried steak, milk gravy, hash browns, toast and eggs.

He thought he'd probably ruined her appetite, but she picked up her fork and, after one tentative bite, dug in. As he watched her, he couldn't help smiling. He liked a woman with a healthy appetite. He liked Levi. The thought brought with it a wave of dread. *Don't get this woman killed.*

"Seth Gantry?" cried a plump, elderly woman as she neared their table.

He rose to give her a hug. "This is my friend, Levi," he said, and offered Teresa a seat.

She declined. "Can't now. I've got two dozen pies going there in the kitchen. When did you get back?"

"Yesterday."

"I guess I don't need to ask what you're doing here now," she said, sounding unhappy about it. "I figured you'd show up not long after Alex did."

"Do you know where he might be staying?"

She shook her head. "He's doing dishes at Chico. That's all I can tell you. You aren't looking for trouble, are you, Seth?"

He shook his head and gave her a smile. "You know me, Teresa."

"Yeah, that's what worries me." She smiled at him and not unkindly. "It's nice to see you back in town, no matter what your reason. I suppose you heard about Wally's accident."

He nodded, noticing the way she said the word "accident." He suspected everyone in town thought it an odd coincidence that Wally Stanley would wheel himself down his office stairs just after Alex got out of prison.

"Have you heard how he's doing this morning?" she asked, concern in her voice.

"Still unconscious." Seth knew how close Teresa and Wally were. He'd often wondered why they'd never married.

Teresa shifted her gaze to Levi. "Nice meeting you. Come back for some pie later. My treat."

Seth watched Teresa return to the kitchen, thinking about Alex. He'd once been a top architect in the area. Now he was a felon out on parole doing dishes at Chico Hot Springs Resort. Alex deserved worse for killing Shanna, but still Seth felt sad for his former friend.

When Seth turned back to the table, he found Levi staring behind her, intent on something in the parking lot. He felt a jolt when she whirled around to face him and he saw her scared expression. "What is it?"

"I just saw a red stock truck," Levi whispered. "It turned into the lot."

Chapter Eleven

Seth dropped a twenty onto the table and got to his feet. "Come on, I know the back way out of here."

"I'm sure you do." She took one last bite of her breakfast and let him lead her through the kitchen and out into the late morning.

"I think we should take a little walk," he said, latching onto her arm as they crossed the street.

Seth glanced back once they'd reached the other side. A red stock truck was parked in the café lot and it looked exactly like the one he'd seen last night in Big Timber.

He pulled Levi into an antique store and waited, hoping to catch a glimpse of the driver as he entered the café. But Seth didn't see anyone go in and suddenly felt conspicuous staring out the window. He and Levi would kill a little time in here, then go looking for Alex. One thing was for sure, Alex wouldn't be driving a stock truck.

It probably wasn't even the same stock truck anyway, he thought as he moved around the store, pretending to shop. He was just being nervous, jumping at shadows.

Levi picked up a lamp and inspected it with obvious interest. Women, they could shop anytime, anywhere, under any circumstances. She turned to show him the lamp. The base was an old boot, the shade stamped with brands. Her taste in lamps surprised him a little because he actually liked the lamp.

Suddenly her eyes widened, her gaze not on him anymore but behind him, just over his right shoulder.

He spun fast, but not fast enough. Two powerful arms grabbed him, crushing the air from his lungs as he was picked off his feet and spun around.

The man who had him in a bear hug let out a bellow. "You son of a cross-eyed prairie dog!"

"No!" Seth yelled as he spotted Levi coming fast, the lamp raised in one hand and a look of fury in her eyes, her intended point of impact seemingly the man's head. "He's my brother!"

She stopped and slowly lowered the lamp. "Your brother?"

Cody Gantry grinned and dropped Seth to the floor.

"My *little* brother," Seth said. Cody was at least four inches taller and a lot broader. "I have two more like him at home. Only they're bigger."

"You know I thought I saw you last night in Big Timber, of all places," Cody said, squinting at him. "I almost stopped but then, well, I told myself I must be imagining things. What would my big brother be doing in a phone booth in Big Timber kissing some good-looking woman? So what *are* you doing in town? Why haven't you been out to the ranch yet?"

Seth shot a look at Levi. "I'm on a job."

Cody finally followed Seth's gaze to Levi. He broke into a big grin. "If we could all have jobs like you, big brother. About that phone booth—"

"Levi, meet my brother Cody."

Her hand disappeared into Cody's large one. Seth watched his brother's face. Did he see the resemblance to Shanna?

"Home?" Levi asked, turning to look at Seth.

"My family owns a place outside of town," he said.

"Make him bring you out to the place," Cody told Levi, then looked at Seth again, his expression serious. "The folks would really like to see you."

Seth nodded. "The thing is…I'm kinda in a bind, right now, with this job. After it's over—"

Cody looked down at his boots for a moment, then up at Levi. "There's something you have to understand about my brother. He has to do everything on his own. Which means the hardest way there is." All the teasing left his voice as he turned back to Seth. "But if you need some help, you know we're here for you." Had he heard Alex had been released?

"Thanks, little brother," Seth said, stepping into his brother's hug. "There *is* one thing you can do for me. There's an old green International Harvester pickup parked two streets over. I'd appreciate it if you could get it back up the Boulder. That last place before you reach the natural bridge."

Cody grinned. "Let me guess, I'm not going to find the keys in it, right?" He shook his head. "Some things just never change." He reached out to squeeze Seth's shoulder. "Don't worry, I'll take care of it."

"Park it in the barn, if you would," Seth added.

"You got it." He held Seth's gaze for a long moment. "We've all missed you, Seth. I hope we can expect you for Christmas." He didn't wait for a response. He tipped his hat to Levi. Then took one last look at Seth. "Take care of yourself."

As Seth watched his brother leave, he realized how much he'd missed his family. If nothing else, Alex had brought him home. But for how long?

LEVI WATCHED CODY CROSS the street to the stock truck that had followed them the night before, then turned her gaze on Seth. "You have family here." Even to her ears, it sounded more like an accusation than a statement of fact.

"Yeah. I told you I grew up around here," Seth said as he took the lamp from her and put it back. "If we live through this, I'll buy the lamp for you. In the meantime, let's get out of here before someone else I know shows up."

"Why didn't you tell me you had family here?" she demanded as they left the store.

He kept walking. "What did you think? That I just crawled out from under a rock?"

"You know darned well what I thought," she snapped. "Don't you think it's time you told me something about yourself?"

"Right now? This can't wait until a time when we aren't busy?"

"We aren't that busy." She wasn't going to let him put her off. Not this time.

"You do pick your moments," he grumbled. "I grew up on a ranch in Paradise Valley just south of here. The Double Bar G. After high school I moved into town.''

''You didn't go to college?'' she asked, surprised.

''Not until later.'' He crossed the street.

She went after him. She had to trot to keep up with his long legs and she knew he thought he could outwalk her questions. How wrong he was. ''Before or after you became a private investigator?''

''Before.'' Before Shanna?

''What did you study in college?''

''Ranch management.'' He smiled over at her. ''Surprised?''

He knew she was. She could hear the satisfaction in his voice. He liked surprising her as much as she did him. ''Your brothers work the ranch?''

He nodded and kept walking.

''And your parents?'' she asked, phrasing her question so he had to do more than nod.

Seth stopped so suddenly she almost crashed into him. He turned to face her. ''They're both still alive and live at the ranch. My brothers are all bachelors, all younger, all more handsome, bigger and more talented than me. Anything else?''

''No sisters?''

''One, a spitfire like you,'' he said. ''Casey's the youngest. She'd like you.''

Levi shot him a look. She wasn't sure that was a compliment. ''Why would a rancher become a private investigator?''

''Seems obvious enough.'' He stopped and held open a door for her. ''I planned to return to ranching someday.''

It wasn't until she stepped into the building and caught a whiff of stale beer that she realized he'd brought her to a bar. It was dark and smoky, only the twinkle of neon beer signs behind the bar providing any light.

Seth went to the bar and sat down on one of the stools. She followed him, wondering what they were doing now.

"Do you want a beer, or something stronger?" he asked as she climbed up onto the stool next to him.

"Isn't it a little early to start drinking?" she asked. Then lowering her voice, she said, "Don't you dare tell me this is your plan. Getting drunk."

"I never get drunk," he said indignantly.

There were several men at the other end of the bar, two guys playing pool in the back and a couple at one of the tables.

"Whatcha gonna have?" the bartender asked as he slid two cocktail napkins in front of them.

"A Coke," Levi said, grimacing at the dead animal heads hanging on the walls.

"Whatever you've got on tap," Seth said.

She waited until the bartender left before she asked quietly, "Just exactly what *are* we doing?"

Seth only grinned.

When the bartender brought their drinks, Seth asked, "Haven't seen Alex Wells around, have you?" His voice was loud enough that every head in the place turned toward them, even the couple at the table who'd been busy mooning over each other.

The bartender carefully set down their drinks. "Alex Wells?" He shot a glance down the bar at the fellows nursing their Bloody Marys, then shook his head.

"That was smooth," she said to Seth after the

bartender left. "Are you planning to do this in every bar in Livingston?"

Seth pushed back his Stetson, tossed some money onto the bar and, leaving his beer untouched, slid off his stool. "You bet I am," he said, dragging her back out into the daylight.

Fortunately, he was exaggerating. They hit only two other bars. He made a phone call at the last one before he took her back to the Blazer.

"I called the hospital," he said, once they were moving.

"How's Wally?" she asked, suddenly afraid.

"The same." He shifted.

"Have you changed your mind?" she asked.

He glanced over at her and frowned as if he'd missed something, then returned to his driving. She noted that they seemed to be headed for the river.

He swung his gaze slowly back to her. A grin curled his mustache. "You just don't know when to quit, do you?"

"I guess not," she admitted. "It's just that under the circumstances don't you think I ought to know some things about you?"

"What circumstances are those?" He gave her an innocent grin.

"I swear there's something you don't want me to find out," she said, only half joking.

When he didn't answer, she looked over at him. He was staring straight ahead, the grin long gone. My God, how many secrets did the man have?

"Don't try to figure me out, Levi," he said after a moment, all the humor gone from his voice. "I'm just not that complex or that interesting."

"Sorry to disappoint you, but I've already figured you out. It's not that tough," she lied.

He shook his head, not taking the bait, and she knew that was all she would get out of him now.

She looked up as he pulled into what, according to the sign, was the Park County Fairgrounds.

She hated to ask.

"You want a gun, don't you?" he said in answer to her frown, then pointed to a sign hanging over the door of one of the livestock barns. Gun Show.

Inside, she followed Seth past table after table of rifles, handguns, assault weapons and western memorabilia. He bought her a detective special .38 with a shoulder holster and some special shells that the vendor promised would stop an intruder in his tracks.

"You might as well carry your gun on you," he said to her. "It won't show under your coat." He watched as she shrugged into the holster, then slipped the pistol into it. The gun nestled against her ribs, giving her a sense of security she liked.

"If you have to, use it," Seth said, eyeing her.

"Thanks," she said, for both the advice and the pistol.

"What now?" she asked as he pulled out of the fairgrounds. "More barhopping?"

"I thought we'd drive out to Chico Hot Springs. Maybe we'll get lucky and find Alex elbow deep in dishwater."

Levi doubted that. Nor did she think Seth expected it, either. It seemed pretty obvious what they were doing. Putting the word out that Seth was looking for Alex. She hoped Seth wasn't making a huge mistake.

He turned just south of town onto a gravel road—Old Yellowstone Trail, according to the sign—that skirted the foothills on the west side of the valley and ran south through farm and ranch land. Only a sifting of snow dusted the foothills, leaving the valley bare and still golden with hay stubble. They passed fields of cows, long rows of round hay bales, aging barns and farm equipment.

Levi saw Seth checking the rearview mirror but she could see no other cars behind them for miles. It didn't, however, take away the feeling that they weren't alone and hadn't been since they'd hit Montana.

As Seth drove, she looked out at the mountains that corralled Paradise Valley. It did look like paradise. The valley was wide and long with fields of grain, pastures dotted with cattle and sheep, a sprinkling of houses. The mountains surrounding the valley shot straight up into towering, craggy, snow-capped peaks. There was nothing like it in Texas.

The thought surprised her. Born and bred a Texan, she'd never thought any other place would appeal to her the way this one did. Was it the place, she wondered, or the man next to her?

She sneaked a look at him. What was it about Seth Gantry, sex appeal aside, that she found so blamed interesting? She didn't know. He was a puzzle. A mystery. It didn't help that she felt there was something he was trying very hard to keep from her.

Not that he'd bothered to tell her much about himself. Why did it surprise her that he had a ranch and family here? Probably because he'd left everything behind to move to Texas. Not just his family, but his roots. He obviously loved his family, this country, even that windy town of Livingston behind them.

She caught him looking longingly off to the southeast, but she could see nothing except foothills backed up by mountains.

"You said your family ranch is in this valley?" she asked, drawing his dark eyes to her.

He nodded. "Up that way." He motioned to the spot he'd been eyeing and turned his attention back to his driving. "By Dailey Lake."

She looked out at the land. From the Yellowstone River bottom and the thick stands of cottonwoods, the land ran to rolling farm and ranch land, to rocky bluffs, dark green pines and finally the upward sweep of the tall, rugged mountains. Yes, she could see him growing up here. It suited him. Even the wind. There was that same wild, untamed feel about him. Just like the land he so obviously loved.

CHICO HOT SPRINGS RESORT rested at the base of Chico Peak. The old hotel was straight out of a western with its white lap siding, dark green trim and tiny dormer windows looking out on the mountains, and its rustic log interior.

Levi wandered through the long dining room to the kitchen.

"Didn't show for work," the man in a chef's hat informed Seth when he inquired about Alex. "Not yesterday. Or today."

In the bar, Seth got the same answer. No Alex Wells. Levi looked out at the large outdoor pool, steam rising off the water, and worried they were on a wild-goose chase.

"Well, that about covers that," Seth said as they got back into the Blazer.

"Now what?" she asked, looking down toward the valley.

He glanced over at her, obviously aware of all the times she'd asked that very question. "One more stop."

DUSK HAD SETTLED into the cottonwoods along the Yellowstone as Seth drove down to Emigrant and the Old Saloon. Emigrant had once been a train stop but was now little more than a flashing yellow light along the highway. There was a gas station, small grocery, laundry, bar and café.

Seth stopped in front of the bar and Levi groaned.

This bar was pretty much like the rest they'd been in that day. Rustic. Western. And occupied with locals. The locals always looked up when she and Seth walked in.

Because of the time of day, the place was about half-full. Seth ordered a beer, Levi a Coke. They sat sipping their drinks, the day dying outside the door.

As short as the day had been, it seemed long. Maybe because she felt she'd been looking over her shoulder the whole time.

Seth's inquiry as to Alex Wells caused the usual rapt attention—and silence. If anyone knew where Alex was, they weren't talking. But she got the feeling that everyone in the bar knew the name, probably the story, as well.

She and Seth ordered dinner and moved into the café side of the bar to eat a steak that Levi swore was as big as a saddle and a potato as large as her head. The food tasted wonderful and Seth seemed to relax a little, although he never stopped watching the door or the other customers who wandered in.

They talked about ranching, horses, bulls they'd like to buy, livestock they'd like to raise. Dream stuff. It felt good. Seth actually liked to listen to Levi, when she wasn't grilling him about his past. She was funny and amusing, interesting and intelligent and she knew a lot about ranching. He liked her enthusiasm. He liked her mouth. He liked her. More than he wanted to.

He tried not to think about the past. About Shanna. Or Alex. Or the future. He felt restless for the first time in eight years and he knew coming back here had caused at least part of it. Levi had caused even more of it. Because she'd resembled Shanna so much at first, or because she was like no woman he'd ever met before?

Either way, it scared him, because he knew now more than ever that he hadn't put the past to rest. Not by a long shot. And until he did, he had no future.

When they'd finished eating, he went to the bar to pay their bill.

"Just a moment," the bartender said after taking the money. He handed Seth a folded piece of paper.

"Who gave you this?" Seth asked, glancing down the bar.

"That older man who was sitting at the far end of the bar. He left just a few minutes ago, but he asked me to give you this."

Seth opened the note and read the barely legible scrawl: *"Heard you asking about Alex. Meet me outside. Around back."*

AN ELDERLY MAN CAME OUT of the darkness the moment Seth and Levi rounded the side of the bar. Stooped and haggard, he stared at them through rheumy eyes and motioned for them to follow.

The pending nightfall burrowed deep shadows between the buildings. Seth pulled Levi close to him as he let the old man draw them deeper into the cold blackness wedged between the two buildings.

"You the fella who was asking about Alex Wells?" the man asked, stopping short of the back of the building. He stood silhouetted against the lighter night sky behind him.

"Yes," Seth replied, and waited, sensing the old man's hesitancy, knowing that he recognized them or he wouldn't have motioned them back here. Was he just being careful?

"Alex weren't so bad," the man said after a moment, "when he was younger, but now—" His gaze moved to Levi. "Why are you looking for him?"

"I think he's involved in a possible murder scheme," Seth said, going for broke.

The man was still looking at Levi. "Involving her?"

Seth nodded, drawing the man's gaze back to him. The old guy knew something or he wouldn't have made the connection. "How do you know Alex?"

"I'm his uncle by marriage. Name's Bergstrom. Delbert Bergstrom."

Seth remembered a distant relative at Alex's trial. The rest of Alex's family had long since moved away. Seth studied the uncle. The past eight years hadn't been kind to Delbert Bergstrom.

"Made some bad friends at prison, Alex did,"

Delbert said. "Going to get himself in real trouble this time, ain't he?"

Sam wondered at the notion that the first murder hadn't been real trouble. "We need to know just what Alex is involved in so we can stop it," Seth said. "If you can help us…"

Delbert scratched his fuzzing grayed jaw for a moment. "I found some papers after he disappeared."

Disappeared? "He was staying with you?"

The uncle nodded. "Up until a few days ago. Left without a word. No one's seen him."

"What kind of papers?" Seth asked.

"Plans, you know, names, phone numbers, people he's fallen in with," Delbert said, and shook his head.

"I'd like to see those papers," Seth said.

"I kinda thought you might. There is just one thing. When you find him, I want your promise that you'll get him to the law if you can," Delbert said. "I used to be quite fond of the boy. I hate to see him get hisself killed."

"You have my word," Seth said. He didn't want Alex's blood on his hands. He just wanted him safe behind bars again.

"Meet me at the Blue Goose in Gardiner. Tomorrow. About eleven. I'll bring the papers."

"Why not just get us the papers tonight?" Seth asked quickly.

Delbert shook his head. "Tomorrow." He turned and disappeared around the corner of the building. Seth looked over at Levi. She hadn't said a word the entire time, he realized. He wasn't sure why, but it made him smile.

"He loves Alex," she said as they walked back through the darkness to the parking lot. "He thinks maybe he can save him."

Seth didn't say anything. He suspected that Delbert was giving Alex one more night to turn up and explain the papers. Otherwise, he would give the incriminating documents to Seth and Levi tomorrow.

Seth just hoped that Delbert's love for his nephew didn't get him killed. Who knew whom Alex had fallen in with. The attempted murder of a senator's—soon to possibly be president's—daughter was big time and, convicted killer or not, Alex was out of his league.

In the phone booth outside the bar, Seth phoned Jerilyn on a safe line. She answered on the first ring.

"I was worried you wouldn't call," she said.

He heard her take a long drag on her cigarette. "I need you to run a name for me. Alex Wells. He just got out of prison on parole. I need to know when he got out, where he's been, especially anyone he might have befriended at prison."

"You got it," she said, sounding strange. "Anything else?"

"No. How are things there?"

"Fine."

He didn't believe it. She sounded upset.

"Anything more on the armored car robbery?"

"Not that I've heard. No more odd phone calls, either. I'm just worried about you," she said at last. "Will you call me tonight?"

Seth glanced over at Levi. "No. In the morning."

"Seth?"

"Yeah?"

"Are you having any luck getting to the bottom of this?"

"Maybe. Levi and I just met Alex Wells's uncle, Delbert Bergstrom. He seems to think he might know something. We meet with him tomorrow morning."

"Levi?" she asked.

"It's a nickname."

"Seth, I'm worried about you."

"Don't be," he said. "I think we're getting close. Hopefully by this time tomorrow it will be over."

"Good. I'll talk to you in the morning then," she said, sounding a little better.

He hung up to find Levi staring across the highway at the gas station and grocery. Several cars were parked on the side, but the glare of the outside lights on the large windows made it hard to see faces inside.

"Someone's out there watching us, isn't he," Levi said.

Seth nodded, glad he wasn't the only one to feel it. It gave him even more faith in her intuition, in her intelligence. "I think we've been followed all day." Not that he'd ever seen a tail, but either he was getting more paranoid or someone had been watching them. Was still watching them. And it wasn't Delbert Bergstrom.

"Let's get out of here," he said as they walked to the Blazer.

Seth was glad he'd gotten Levi a gun. But she was wrong about one thing. He wasn't worried about Alex taking it away from her and using it on her. Alex wouldn't need Levi's gun. In fact, Seth would stake his life on Alex not using any gun if he ever got the chance alone with an unarmed Levi. Seth just hoped to hell that Levi would use the gun if she had to.

"Do you think the papers will help us find Alex?" she asked when he joined her inside the car.

Seth shrugged. "It's worth a chance. At least we'll know what's going on. And hopefully who's involved." He watched her bite at her lower lip and felt a wave of desire wash over him, drowning him in need. Tonight, he thought, he wasn't about to risk that Alex might decide to strike. He wasn't about to risk Levi. To hell with Alex tonight. Seth much preferred to face him in the daylight anyway.

The truth was, Seth wanted Levi alone. Just for tonight. Tomorrow he and Levi would meet Delbert Bergstrom at the Blue Goose in Gardiner. The papers might prove to be nothing. He'd take tomorrow as it came, but tonight...well, tonight, he just wanted to be with Levi someplace safe, someplace away from everything and everyone.

"What would you say if I told you we were going to lose whoever is following us?" he asked her. "At least for tonight?"

She looked up at him, her violet eyes bright and shiny. "I'd like that. Can you do it?"

"You forget," he said as he started the Blazer, "I'm a trained professional."

She laughed with him as he drove south toward Gardiner and Yellowstone Park.

Seth hadn't gone far when he picked up the tail. He smiled to himself. It had been a while since he'd had a good car chase. In this rig, he knew he could lose whoever was following them. He grinned over at Levi. "Buckle up and hang on, princess. We're going for a ride."

NIGHT SLIPPED down from the mountains to pool, dark and cold in the foothills. Clouds cloaked the moon and the stars. Even the wind deserted the darkness.

In the wash of the headlights, Levi watched the countryside sweep past, faster and faster. Behind them, the twin lights stuck to them, hanging back just enough that she couldn't recognize the make of the vehicle.

"What if it's a highway patrol?" she asked, always Little Miss Law-Abiding.

Seth smiled as he put his foot into the gas pedal. "Then expect to see flashing blue and red lights any minute."

Increased speed pressed her to the seat. The Blazer began to float, touching down with a jolt on the pavement as it roared through the night. She glanced over at the speedometer. It was pegged, the needle teetering as far to the right as it could go. The night flashed by. The countryside blurred. The Blazer engine roared like a giant cat, running strong, running fast.

"Get ready for a right-hand turn," Seth announced.

"What?" she cried, and braced herself, although she wondered what the point was at this speed.

They came up over a rise, catching air as the tires left the pavement. The moment the tires touched down again, Seth hit the brakes and the lights. The Blazer went into a skid. The headlights went out; darkness came rushing at them.

Levi's heart leaped up into her throat—which was fortunate since she would have screamed if she could have. The Blazer left the pavement, skidding onto what sounded like gravel and ice.

All she got out was a heartfelt gasp. For several horrifying moments, she could see nothing but blackness. Then a road materialized, faint but distinctly lighter than the dark pines that lined both sides of it.

"This seems a little dangerous." Her voice came out a croak and her hands ached from hanging on so tightly.

"Are you kidding? This is dangerous as hell," Seth said as he barreled down the road in darkness.

She glanced over at him just to make sure he hadn't gone completely insane. Fortunately, it was too dark to tell.

Behind them, she could see nothing. Then a set of headlights blinked like the eyes of a large carnivorous beast tracking them. They flew over a couple of small rises, then dropped down to the river, still going fast and furious.

"So tell me your life story," Seth said as they went airborne on one of the dips in the road.

"You have to be kidding." Her voice sounded as if she'd been running along beside the car. "Now?"

"Come on, you're so interested in my story. What was it like growing up in Texas the daughter of a politician?"

She shot him a look. He really was a madman. Now definitely did not seem like the time for this. Nor would she even be here, on the run and in fear for her life, if she wasn't the daughter of a politician. That should tell him something.

He glanced over at her.

"Don't do that!" she cried. "All right. Growing up on a ranch is the perfect place to be a kid—"

"You want kids?" he asked, his gaze shifting to her for another instant.

"Yes," she answer quickly, afraid he'd look away from the road again.

"How many?"

"A half dozen." She tightened her grip on the dash as the Blazer threw up a wave of gravel on a sharp turn. "Give or take three."

"Great. You don't seem very political to me."

She kept her attention on the road ahead. Someone had to. "What gave you that idea?"

He chuckled. "The distinctly disgusted sound you made when I asked was a dead giveaway."

"I hate politics."

"Oh, come on, growing up with a Texas state senator?" he said as the Blazer roared down another hill.

"Believe me." She felt that old defensiveness when the subject came up. "My father loves politics. Loves it all." She shrugged but still held onto the dash for dear life. "Someone had to run the ranch with him gone all the time. I got the job."

"You make it sound as if you had no choice," Seth said. "I'm sure your father could have hired someone to run the Altamira if you didn't want to."

Another sore point. The man had honed in on them as unerring as a SCUD missile.

"I care too much about the ranch," she said. "I also remember when I was a kid and Daddy hired a man from his unit in Vietnam. The man stole the ranch blind before he got caught." She shook her head. "My father's priorities aren't the Altamira. So mine were."

Seth lifted one dark brow. "Were?"

Why had she used the past tense? Because the Altamira and that life seemed like a lifetime ago? Or because she'd changed? Changed because of this experience. Or because of this man?

She realized they were still flying low to the ground and she couldn't see any lights behind them anymore. "I think you're enjoying this a little too much," she said, her eyes fixed on the darkness ahead, praying that nothing but road appeared in front of them.

Seth chuckled and kept driving. The narrow gravel road forked, turned into a narrower rutted dirt road, forked again and turned into a jeep trail. Fortunately by that time, he had slowed the Blazer considerably and turned the headlights back on.

"I think you lost them," she said, looking back. She let out a relieved sigh and pried her fingers off the dash.

"That was the idea," he said. In the dash lights she could see his satisfied grin. "What do you think?"

She knew what he was asking. She was impressed with his driving. With him. Really impressed. She'd pretty much decided that this man could do anything. But she hated to give him the satisfaction of admitting it. "Not bad."

"Not bad?" he echoed.

"All right," she relented. "You could use some work on your turns, but you drive fairly well."

"Thanks," he said dryly. "I'll try not to let it go to my head."

"It's probably too late for that." She smiled at him as he slowed even more. Their gazes touched as tentatively as a caress, and just as intimate.

He turned back to his driving. In the distance she could make out a huge barn set back in the pines ,and rocks. She couldn't see any other buildings, no other signs of civilization or of life. They had to be miles from the highway and even farther from the nearest town.

Seth pulled off on a more rugged road in the direction of the barn. "I hope you don't mind, but this is the safest place I could think of to spend the night," he said as he pulled the Blazer into a stand of trees, hiding it from view of the road. "And the most secluded."

"It's perfect." More perfect than he could know, she thought. She loved barns. And right now she really liked the idea of seclusion.

As she opened her door and got out, she spotted one solitary star. It escaped the clouds to glitter pure white against the dark sky. The wish came out of nowhere. A spur-of-the-moment wish. A heartfelt wish that, until she made it, she hadn't realized how much she wanted, needed, it to come true.

Levi glanced over at Seth. A shaft of moonlight broke through the clouds to bathe them in silver. As her gaze met Seth's across the hood of the car, she realized with a jolt of surprise—and pleasure—this was one wish that actually might come true. Desire blazed in his eyes, brighter than all the stars in the galaxy.

"Let's go see what we have for accommodations," he said, and reached for her hand.

Suddenly the whole sky seemed brimming with

starlight. As she put her hand in his, Levi felt safer than she'd ever felt. A strange sensation, to say the least, especially under the circumstances.

He walked only a few steps and stopped. "Have you ever seen anything like that sky?" he asked, and glanced over at her.

His gaze lit her with desire and heat and a lightness that seemed to lift her off her feet. What had happened to the woman who prided herself on keeping both feet firmly on the ground?

And yet, she felt no fear. Just excitement. Eagerness. Elation at the very thought of what was to come.

He lowered his lips to hers. At first tentatively, teasing, tasting, tempting her. It didn't take much temptation. She felt he was holding back. Because he still hadn't gotten over Shanna? Or because he was afraid of being hurt again? She couldn't imagine Seth Gantry being afraid. Not really.

He pulled back a little from the kiss. The moonlight lit his face for just an instant. Well, how about that. Banked in the depths of all that black-eyed darkness was honest-to-goodness fear. She knew the look.

She smiled and, hooking her arms around his neck, pulled him down to her mouth again. Not surprisingly, that seemed to be all the prompting he needed. He kissed her, really kissed her, convincing her that anything he did, he did well.

His kiss was hard and hot. It liquefied her limbs until she was clinging desperately to him. He swung her up into his arms and shoved open the barn door. Levi had never felt such an urge to rejoice. Until this moment.

The barn was dark. It took a few seconds for her eyes to adjust. But Seth seemed to have night vision as he carried her deep inside. Moon- and starlight dropped in through a window in the haymow, spilling onto a pile of fresh hay, like an omen. A blessing. A wish come true.

Seth set her down but didn't let go of her as he pulled a horse blanket from under the saddles lined up along the stall. He tossed the blanket onto the hay and, closing the door, pulled her into his arms, into his kiss.

His mouth was heat and wetness, his lips power and demand, his tongue pure satisfaction.

"Oh, Seth," she breathed against his lips, against the wonderful feel of his mustache, as she fought to catch her breath.

"I want to make love to you, princess," he whispered, his breathing as unsteady as her own. She pressed the palm of her hand to his chest and felt his heart. It answered with an accompanying beat.

She smiled up into his dark eyes, feeling absolutely no need for words.

Seth returned her smile and slowly drew her down onto the blanket in a nest of sweet-scented hay. The starlight overhead glittered like a sprinkling of fairy dust. Nothing could have made the night more magical. Or the man who took her in his arms more wondrous.

There was nothing Seth Gantry couldn't do. And astoundingly well.

Chapter Twelve

Seth lay beside Levi, watching her sleep. He was starting to make a habit of this, he realized. But he liked watching her. Asleep, she definitely looked angelic. This morning she looked more beautiful than he thought he'd ever seen her. There was a warm softness to her, a contentment, a peacefulness about her. If this was what lovemaking did for her, she ought to do it more often.

Making love to her had been nothing short of amazing. He still felt awestruck by it.

He found himself wondering about Levi, about the small things, large things, things he'd never thought about with any other woman. Not even Shanna. He wanted to know everything about Levi. He smiled, remembering all the questions she'd asked him and wondered— No, she was just worried about the man she was risking her life with.

He looked up at the sunlight streaming down through the rafters and knew they had to get going. But he didn't want to wake her. He didn't want to leave this barn. He'd much prefer pulling her closer, burying his face in her warmth, making love to her again and again.

But making love to her had left him even more confused. He squeezed his eyes closed for a moment to chase away the thoughts. Thoughts of Shanna. Thoughts of Levi. Both were all tangled into a knot of heartache.

He wanted desperately to tell Levi how he felt. About her and about Shanna. But how could he explain those feelings when he didn't understand them yet himself?

All he knew was that making love to Levi had changed something inside him. But Alex was still out there and Seth still had to face his past. For the first time in eight years, though, he felt ready. Because of Levi.

Once he knew that Levi was safe and Alex was behind bars again, then he'd face his feelings.

One thing Seth knew for sure. He couldn't let the woman in the bed of hay or the way he felt about her dictate what he did next. If he did, he'd get them both killed. But at the same time, he didn't want to take any chances with her life. He'd worried that once he'd taken her in his arms and made love to her it would change everything. Well, it had.

Now all he had to do was find Alex and keep Levi safe. No small task.

LEVI AWOKE TO FIND SETH staring down at her, his brows furrowed, his eyes dark and troubled.

"Sorry," he said. "But all bets are off. I'm putting you on the next plane. Wherever it's going, that's where you're going."

She laughed and reached up to brush a kiss across

his mouth. She heard his sharp intake of breath, saw desire flame again in his dark eyes.

"I can't take a risk with your life, Levi," he said firmly. "I have to get you out of here. Out of Montana."

"That's crazy, Seth," she said softly. "How do you know that Alex won't be on that plane? Or come after me the moment I'm alone?"

"Dammit, Levi, I can't take a chance with your life. Not after...last night." His gaze softened.

She reached up to cup his bristled jaw in the palm of her hand and gently brushed the pad of her thumb over his lips, his mustache. "I feel the same way you do. I don't want you risking your life. For me. For anything. But, Seth, nothing has changed since yesterday."

"The hell it hasn't," he growled. He drew her thumb to his lips for a kiss.

"Alex or someone is still after us," she reasoned. "You were right in wanting to find him rather than the other way around. If anything, I want more than ever to get this over with." She almost added, "So we can sort our feelings out." But she didn't. She didn't believe her feelings needed sorting. She just wasn't so sure about Seth's. Would he ever get over Shanna? Or would a dead woman always haunt him, always be there between them?

He sucked her thumb into his mouth, his tongue caressing it, his eyes closing. He moaned, his eyes flicked open; he extracted her thumb from his mouth, planted a small kiss on the pad, then returned it to her. "You're right." He pushed himself to his feet. "Maybe Delbert really will be of some help."

He offered her a hand up. But as she rose, he

pulled her into his arms. His kiss was possessive, demanding, questioning. She answered with her lips, her body, her heart.

"I want you, Levi," he breathed against her mouth as he pressed his body over hers and she opened to him, like a flower to the sun. What he didn't realize was that he already had her. Heart, body and soul.

As LEVI WAS GETTING dressed, her stomach growled. Seth grinned at her. "Hungry?"

She nodded and smiled. "Starved."

He felt the same way but didn't like the idea of going into Gardiner for breakfast before they met Delbert. It felt too dangerous.

"I know just the place," he said. "Serves the best food you've ever eaten. And the company ain't bad, either."

She raised a brow but he only grinned.

They passed a few horses and barns and houses before he drove up the side of the mountain and stopped in front of a quaint little house overlooking the valley. "Welcome to Chris and Lise's."

The door flew open about then and a blond woman let out a cry. Two seconds later, the woman was hugging Seth. "Where have you been?" she cried. "I've missed you so much. How dare you stay away for so long."

She turned her jovial face to Levi. "And just who do you have with you? Where did you get this beautiful woman?" Levi found herself in the woman's warm hug before Seth could even get introductions out. "Come on in," Lise cried. "You both look starved."

"We are," Seth admitted.

"You also look as if you spent the night in a barn," she said, pulling a piece of hay from Levi's hair with a broad wink.

"We did," Seth admitted.

"You can tell me why you've stayed away so long while I whip you up some breakfast. Levi looks like she might like a hot shower. Chris is around here somewhere. Chris! We've got company!"

Levi couldn't remember a more wonderful breakfast or more warm and congenial hosts. The hot shower hit the spot, but nothing like Seth's friends. Levi felt she'd known them her whole life and was sorry to leave, promising to return, a promise she hoped she could keep.

"I like your friends," she said as they left.

"I thought you would," Seth said, and smiled at her. "They liked you, too."

"You called Jerilyn," she said, her smile fading along with her good mood.

Seth nodded. "She didn't have a lot. But it seems that Alex befriended a guard at the prison by the nickname of Lars. She's trying to get more."

Levi looked at the towering mountains and the narrow canyon ahead with alarm. "I thought we were going to Gardiner?"

"We are."

"Isn't there a real road to it?" she asked, her concern growing as Seth drove toward what appeared to be a cliff overlooking the river.

He laughed. "This is the back road to Gardiner and Yellowstone Park. I know how fond you are of back roads."

"Seth, this is not a road."

"It just happens to be the first road through Yankee Jim Canyon to Yellowstone Park, named after the man who built it. Before that there was only a trail to Yellowstone."

"Seth, this is still a trail, no matter what Yankee Jim called it." She peered down at the river through Seth's side window and felt queasy. The "road" was nothing more than a narrow, rocky, rutted dual path cut into the cliff over the river.

"Good thing Yankee Jim isn't still around," Seth said, grinning at her. "He used to charge a toll to use this road."

"People actually paid money to drive on this?" she cried.

Seth laughed. "Back before four-wheel-drive vehicles."

Levi shook her head, trying to imagine coming over this in the first cars as she eyed the precarious drop to the river below. The deep green water, fringed with ice, wound through huge boulders in the tight canyon below.

She breathed a sigh of relief when Yankee Jim Canyon opened up into a river valley. The road widened some and, still following the river, wound its way into the backside of Gardiner, Montana, and Yellowstone Park. As they passed the Gardiner High School, Levi saw a herd of elk feeding on the football field. Across the river, more elk lunched on the grass at the Gardiner Baptist Church front lawn. They passed under the arch and into Gardiner with Levi hoping they'd find Delbert Bergstrom waiting for them.

IT WAS TWO MINUTES to eleven when Seth held open the door to the Blue Goose Bar in Gardiner for Levi.

The Blue Goose, or just "The Goose" as locals called it, sat on Park Street. The town was built on the edge of the river. Most of the buildings clung to the side of the canyon. But The Goose, with its red-rock front, faced Yellowstone Park.

The bar was narrow and dark, the only illumination from the two small front windows. A few locals were gathered around the television, watching football. Seth and Levi sat down on one of the log stools and ordered glasses of draft. Delbert Bergstrom wasn't anywhere in sight.

At the back of the bar, a large black woodstove cranked out waves of heat. The bartender, a woman wearing a crop top and bib overalls, slid two beers in front of them.

A half-dozen men were sitting at the bar, none of whom Seth recognized. Either Delbert Bergstrom wasn't here yet. Or he wasn't coming at all.

Seth motioned to the phone booth at the back. He called the hospital first only to find out that Wally was still unconscious, his condition guarded. Then Seth dialed the number Senator McCord had given him. McCord answered on the second ring. The conversation was short. Levi was safe for the moment, Wally was unconscious, Seth hadn't found out anything yet. He didn't tell him about Alex. It was too soon.

McCord said Levi's missing security guards had turned up. All four of them had been waylaid, handcuffed and locked in the trunks of their cars. They all said they hadn't seen the attackers. McCord said he'd fired them, but suspected at least one, if not two, had to have been in it. He'd reached a dead end.

Seth put Levi on the line and left the two of them to talk in private. At the bar, he nursed his beer. It was the last thing he wanted. He wished Delbert would show up. The bar felt too confined, the smell of stale beer too strong, the temperature too hot and stuffy. He felt irritable and restless.

It was a while before Levi rejoined him. She slid up onto the stool next to him and doodled in the condensation on the glass.

"What?" he finally asked. After this many hours with the woman, he knew when something was bothering her.

"Why didn't you tell me about the armored car robbery?"

Her words hit him like a pitched brick.

"It was just the grand finale of a string of bad luck I've been having," he said carefully. "It didn't seem important."

Her gaze flicked over at him. "Not important? An eleven-million-dollar loss?"

He studied her. "What did your father tell you?"

"That you're being investigated."

That didn't come as a surprise to him. But by the scared look on her face, he knew there was more to it. "What else?"

Her gaze slid away. "Some of the money has turned up in an account in your name in a bank in the Caymans."

"The Caymans?" He shook his head, figuring there'd be an arrest warrant out for him the moment he surfaced. Great. How could his luck get any worse? He didn't want to answer that. "Do you think I did it? Robbed the armored car I was intrusted to protect?''

''I know there's something you've been keeping from me,'' she said stubbornly.

''Look at me.'' He cupped her chin in his hand and gently turned her to face him. ''I had nothing to do with the robbery.'' He saw a flicker of belief in her eyes. ''Someone is trying to set me up.''

''Who?'' she asked softly. ''It couldn't have been Alex. He was in prison at the time of the robbery.''

She's already figured that out. He wished now that he'd told her everything, about the robbery, all of his bad luck. But it was too late. He saw suspicion in her eyes and he knew the only way he'd ever have her trust would be to find out who was behind this. Then come clean with her about everything. Even Shanna. Especially Shanna.

''It has to be Alex, even from prison,'' Seth said. ''But I have to be honest with you, Levi, I don't know anymore. I really thought Alex would have taken the bait by now. I'm not sure what to think.''

She nodded and he could tell that his explanation fell short.

''You told your brother Cody yesterday that you weren't going to involve the family again,'' she said tentatively. ''What was that about?''

It was hard to admit what he'd done. ''I'd already had a string of bad luck before I got the armored car job. I needed that job to keep the business afloat after everything else had happened. My family put up my part of the ranch as bond.''

''Oh, Seth,'' she said, tears filling her eyes.

''You understand now why I have to find Alex?

He's the only person who hates me enough to do this to me.''

She said nothing, but she held his gaze for a long moment and in her eyes he saw the need to believe him. That was enough. For now.

He glanced at the clock on the wall. It read a quarter past twelve. ''Come on. There's no reason to wait any longer. Let's see if we can find Delbert.''

Seth had parked the car right out front where they could watch it from the bar. He couldn't believe how paranoid he was getting. But there was no longer any doubt that someone was out to get him. The armored car robbery money in an account in his name proved that.

But where did Levi fit in? Or did she? Had the threat against her just been part of the plan to get to him, Seth wondered as he climbed into the Blazer. He looked over at Levi and started the car. No bombs went off. That was always a good sign. He let out the breath he'd been holding.

IT WAS AFTERNOON by the time they reached the Bergstrom place. The property was located about three miles back, off the road between Gardiner and Emigrant. There'd been a farmhouse on it at one time, but the house had burned down. The property now resembled a huge junkyard. From old railroad cars, fire-gutted house trailers and the emptied shells of several school buses to a cluttered maze of farm machinery, wrecked vehicles and acres of rusted parts, the discarded ruins were strewn across the rolling hills.

''I can't believe anyone lives here,'' Levi said, looking up on the hillside.

"Looks like someone does," he said, pointing to the thin, pale smoke that curled up from one of the trailers in the distance.

The road dropped over a couple of hills to the gate to Bergstrom's property, the trailer disappearing behind the rise. The lane up to the place had long since drifted in with snow to the tops of the fence posts, making it impassable. An ancient rusted-out pickup was stuck up to its axles in a drift not far from the gate. The snow, now brown, sunken and wind sculpted, melted in the warm afternoon sunlight. Seth parked at the gate, figuring if that was Delbert's pickup, there was a good chance he was home.

Seth glanced over at Levi. She looked scared. He liked a woman with good sense. He hated having to take her along, but he wasn't about to leave her alone anywhere. At least if she was with him, he could try to protect her if the need arose. And he didn't doubt that the need would eventually arise. Soon. He hoped she was right, that she would use the pistol he'd bought her—just in case.

They walked up through the open hills, the trailer dipping in and out of view. Seth wondered if Alex was also up there, watching them, waiting for them. Alex had to know by now that Seth was looking for him. Maybe he'd put his aging uncle up to this and they were walking into a trap.

But it just didn't seem like something Alex would do. Alex was a lot of things, but he wasn't a coward who'd hide behind an old man. But then again, Seth had never thought Alex could kill, he reminded himself.

The place gave him the creeps. Two mongrel dogs

began to bark loudly from near the trailer the moment he and Levi topped the last hill. With all this racket, there wasn't any way they could sneak up on anyone. But Seth doubted they could have anyway since they'd had to walk out in the open where they were very visible much of the time. Maybe that's the way someone had planned it.

The trailer was half buried by a melting snowdrift, reminding Seth of a cave. Someone had built on a small enclosed porch out of bare weathered wood on the side. Snow, now dirty and brown and as hard as concrete, had funneled around it.

From the lack of tracks, it appeared no one had been out of the house yet this morning. But who knew how long it would take for the snow to fill tracks the way the wind howled up here along this open ridge.

''What an awful place,'' Levi said.

Awfully easy to hide in, Seth thought. It surprised him that Alex had been staying here. But Seth had learned that when the chips were down, blood helped blood.

''No wonder that old man drinks,'' Levi whispered. ''I'd drink too if I lived here.''

He smiled over at her and was hit by that feeling of déjà vu. And doom. He told himself there was no way history was going to repeat itself. Levi wasn't anything like Shanna. But he knew the resemblance was still there enough that Alex would see it.

The thought sent a shot of pure agony through him. He had to get Levi out of this alive. He knew he'd give his own life to save hers if it came to that. This couldn't end as it had before. He assured himself it wouldn't. Levi might look like Shanna but the two women couldn't be more different. Levi was...unique. He smiled to himself at just how unique the woman was and realized he'd stopped walking and Levi was looking at him in alarm.

"What is it?"

He shook his head, unable to find words to explain why he was smiling or how he felt just being around her, let alone how he felt about what they'd shared the night before.

"You're scaring me," she said, looking up into his face.

"Sorry, I don't mean to." He looked down into her violet eyes. Just the sight of her made his heart pound. But how did he feel about this woman? About Shanna? His heart ached with all the unspoken words he needed to say to Shanna. All the unspoken words he hoped to say to Levi. He dragged his gaze away and started to walk toward the trailer again. He had to bury the past once and for all. Because until he did, he had no future. And even then, he wasn't sure what he had to offer a woman like Levi.

"You know that I've suspected for some time that you're a madman," she said quietly as she trailed along beside him again.

"I think you just might be right."

"That's encouraging," she said.

As they neared the trailer, he was struck by such a sense of foreboding that he almost turned back. If he thought he could end this without going up to the trailer, he would have. He'd have walked away. But he knew better. It was as if his whole life had led up to this moment.

Snow melted everywhere, sending rivulets of water cascading down the hillside and making the ground slick where water smoothed the hard snow into ice. The dogs barked. The sun seemed a little less bright as it hung low in the sky.

"Open your coat so you can get to your gun," he said to Levi.

Her eyes widened but she did as he'd instructed.

He studied her a moment longer, then led the way, making a path through the junk. One of the dogs ran at him and tried to nip him, but Seth spooked the mongrel back. The dog eyed them warily and joined the other one to bark and bare their teeth threateningly, at the same time, keeping their distance.

Why didn't Delbert call off his dogs, Seth thought. Because he's not here? But wasn't that his pickup stuck in the snowbank by the road?

Seth banged on the side of the wooden porch and waited. The dogs had disappeared and the snow melted quietly under the low winter sun. He knocked again. No answer. He pushed aside the four-by-eight-foot sheet of plywood that acted as a door and stepped up into the closed-in porch. The tiny space smelled of dead things and he noticed the remains of a deer carcass the dogs had dragged in.

He knocked on the trailer door, watching Levi and beyond her to the hillside of wrecked and ruined things. He knocked once more, then tried the door.

The trailer door opened and he stuck his head in.

The smell inside was even worse than that on the porch. Dirty clothing, old food and something else, an odor that Seth hoped to never smell again. He turned to find Levi right behind him. The dogs had returned and were crouched in the snow, staring intently at the trailer and them. No longer barking. Just watching and waiting.

"I'm not staying out there," Levi said firmly. "It can't be any scarier inside."

Seth wasn't so sure about that. "All right, but stay right by me."

The house looked like that of an elderly man who collected everything. There was junk everywhere. Stacks of old newspapers and magazines, boxes of paperbacks and junk mail, bags of old clothing and bedding overflowed on what little furniture there was in the living room.

As Seth glanced down the hallway toward the kitchen and bedroom, he thought he heard the whine of a snowmobile in the distance. But what he saw lying on the floor just inside the partially opened doorway of the kitchen diverted his attention. He could see a boot sole and part of an ankle. He stepped toward the kitchen, drawn by the sight of the man's leg, as well as the distinct smell of blood.

Delbert Bergstrom lay in a pool of it, an ice pick sticking up out of his chest.

"Stay back," Seth ordered, and turned to see Levi stumble back into the living room.

"Oh, God, who is it?" she cried, peering through the doorway. "Is it Delbert?"

Seth nodded. "He's dead. Looks like he's been that way for a while, too. Are you all right?"

When Levi didn't answer, he looked over his shoulder at her. She stood silhouetted in the doorway, an odd expression on her face. He'd expected to see shock, even repulsion, fear for sure.

What he didn't expect to see was stark, cold terror. Nor did he expect to see a man standing directly behind her.

Seth bolted upright, his hand instinctively going for the pistol inside his coat. But he stopped in midmotion, two good reasons freezing all movement.

The man behind Levi wore the uniform of a Sheriff's Department deputy. However, the uniform was at definite odds with Levi's expression—and the pistol the man held to her temple.

"Well, well, what do we have here?" the deputy asked as he glanced at Seth, then at the body on the floor. "Looks like I caught you in the act. Put your hands up. No quick moves, you hear?"

LEVI WATCHED SETH RAISE his hands, his movements slow, measured, his gaze signaling her not to do anything stupid. That everything was going to be fine. She didn't think so.

"We just found him like this," Seth said quietly.

"You bet," the man said behind her.

That voice. It jarred a memory but not enough to place the voice.

"I think you'll find that he's been dead for quite a while," Seth said reasonably. "If you'd like to check." He moved a little to the left.

The arm that had grabbed her from behind tightened. The barrel of the gun pressed harder into her temple.

"Let's not be hasty," the man said. "How's about we all move to the living room and discuss this?"

He pulled her backward through the trailer. Seth followed, his gaze locked with hers. Just be calm, it said. Just be calm. But she could see the worry in his features.

"Officer, we didn't kill Delbert," Seth said. "If you just take a look at his body, you'll—"

Officer? Levi didn't hear the rest of what Seth said. She heard nothing but a roar in her ears as she caught her reflection in a mirror on the trailer wall. Her reflection—and the man's.

She didn't see anything but his eyes. The cold gray eyes of a lunatic.

The deputy met her gaze in the mirror and smiled. That's when she saw his face. Really saw it. And that's when she knew for certain that she and Seth were in terrible trouble.

Chapter Thirteen

Seth watched helplessly as the deputy kicked a pile of junk off a chair in the living room and shoved Levi down on it. She seemed in shock, her face pale, her eyes wide and dilated.

"This is a mistake," Seth said, trying hard to be reasonable with the cop, something prudent he'd learned the hard way in his youth.

The deputy was a large, strong-looking man in his late forties with a military haircut of graying brown hair and flat gray eyes. It had crossed Seth's mind that he was no officer of the law, seeing as how he had shown up when he did. Something about the way the man moved, his size and shape, felt strangely familiar. Seth suspected he was the man who'd jumped him by the Boulder River just after the blast. But he couldn't be sure. It had been dark and the man had worn a mask.

The deputy leveled his pistol at Seth's chest and motioned for him to take a chair next to Levi. "There is no mistake. Tell him," the man said to Levi.

Seth shot her a look as he sat down a few feet away.

"He's right, Seth," she said, her voice low. "He knows we didn't kill Alex's uncle. That's not why he's here."

The deputy laughed. "You always were the smart one, weren't you, Little Miss McCord?"

Miss McCord? "You know *him?*" Seth exclaimed.

"He's Billy Bob Larson. He served in the same Special Forces A-Team as my father in Vietnam. A twelve-man unit involved in covert maneuvers behind the lines."

Larson? Could this be the "Lars" that Jerilyn had found out about—Alex's prison guard friend?

"After Vietnam, he worked at the Altamira for a while," Levi added.

"Until that bastard McCord fired me," Billy Bob snarled. "All I wanted was an honest day's pay for an honest day's work."

"You weren't looking for work," she snapped. "You were looking for a handout and you know it."

Billy Bob let out a howl. "What would a spoiled rich girl like you know about work? I bet you've never worked a day in your life."

"And you'd lose," Seth said in her defense.

Billy Bob's mouth twisted into a mean smirk as he swung his gaze to Seth. "Slowly remove your coat and toss whatever weapon you've got in there on the floor. Slowly, I said."

Seth complied since there was little else he could do without risking Levi's life. He wanted desperately to get the jump on the cop, but he couldn't, not without the odds being a whole lot better. His pistol clattered to the floor at Billy Bob's feet.

"Now you, little girl," the deputy said. "Or do

you want me to frisk you? I know you have a gun.
I felt it when I had my arm around you.''

Anger blazing in her violet eyes, she pulled the
pistol from the shoulder holster and dropped it next
to Seth's at the man's feet. "Billy Bob is also the
man who attacked me in Wally's office. I recognize
his eyes."

"I wouldn't be making any accusations if I were
you, little girl, especially against a sheriff's deputy,''
he said as he knelt down to pick up the guns, keeping his gun leveled on Seth. He tossed their guns
back into one of the corners filled with junk.
"You're in enough trouble as it is."

Seth fought the anger that raced through his veins
like wildfire. He wanted to get his hands around the
man's throat. "A-Team, huh? You attack women
and men in wheelchairs?"

Billy Bob swore and swung the barrel of the pistol
around so it pointed at Levi's chest. "Listen up,
cowboy. Don't push me or you'll wish you hadn't,
understand? I say sit, you sit. I say shut up, you shut
up. One of you moves, I shoot Little Miss McCord.
Got that?"

"Got it," Seth said, afraid the man would do it.

Billy Bob pulled a cell phone from his uniform
pocket and tapped out a number. Long distance,
from the amount of numbers he dialed. Not that almost any place wasn't long-distance from here, Seth
thought.

Billy Bob watched Seth closely as he waited.
"Yeah. I have a couple of desperadoes I just caught
red-handed," he said into the phone. "Yeah? Make
it quick." He hung up. "Now we wait for backup
to arrive."

"You didn't call the Sheriff's Department for backup," Seth said.

"Oh yeah? How do you know that, Gantry?" the deputy asked belligerently.

Gantry. "Then you know who I am?" Seth said.

"You'd be surprised what I know," he retorted.

"Like where Alex Wells is?" Seth asked. "Is that who we're waiting for?"

Billy Bob just shook his head and sat down on the frayed end of an old couch to wait. "The two of you think you're pretty smart. Problem is, the smart guy is the one with the gun. Any fool knows that."

LEVI HAD TIRED of the man's games and was worried Seth was right. Billy Bob was waiting for Alex and Alex was coming here to kill them.

"What is it you want from us?" she asked, remembering Seth's philosophy. They desperately needed a game plan.

Billy Bob smiled. "Well, now that you ask, I want to be the man who brought down the great James Marshall McCord."

"So this *is* about my father," she said.

"You bet it is," Billy Bob admitted freely. "It's also about liberty, justice and the pursuit of happiness. It's about democracy and equality for all men." He put the hand not holding the gun over his heart and she thought for a moment he might sing "The Star-Spangled Banner." From the look in Seth's eye, it would be the last song Billy Bob Larson ever sang.

"You're crazy," she said, dismissing him with a shake of her head.

"Like a fox," he said, his grin not quite hiding his irritation with her. "I got you, don't I? What do you think your current market value is? Too bad your old man hasn't thrown his hat into the ring for president. That would definitely up the ante."

"If money is all you want—"

"Like money is something to sneer at." He spit into a pile of old clothing beside the couch. "But I want a lot more than money." His expression turned mean. "A whole lot more."

"So much for liberty and justice," she said. "This is really about greed then." She could see Seth out of the corner of her eye, trying to warn her to back off. But hadn't Seth said you couldn't make a plan until you knew what you were facing? Well, it was time they knew exactly what this was about. If Billy Bob even knew.

"How do you expect to get any money out of my father if I'm dead?" she asked. "I could have been killed in that explosion at the cabin."

Billy Bob nodded. "Should have been killed. Good thing I came back to check and happened to see the tracks going up the hillside in the moonlight."

"You were the one who attacked us by the river," Levi said. She noted that he was about the right size, and through his shirt she could see a bandage on his arm where he'd fought with Seth. For his age, the man was formidable.

"This ain't my first rodeo, little girl," Billy Bob said arrogantly. "I knew you'd head for the river. You think all that training in Vietnam was wasted?"

"She's right, there won't be any money in it for you if you kill her," Seth pointed out. "McCord's no fool. He'll demand to speak to her before he pays you one red cent.''

Billy Bob smiled. ''Maybe I just want McCord to suffer.''

''Why do you dislike him so?'' Levi asked, horrified by this man's cruelty. ''I thought he saved your life in Vietnam?''

''You have no idea what my life has been like since. Neither does your daddy,'' Billy Bob said bitterly. ''Oh, Jim pretended to care at first. But why should he help me out? Hell, he was the one who came home the big war hero. I wasn't nothin', just the guy who risked his damned neck over there in those jungles. Ended up with a metal plate in my head. And for what?''

She flinched at the hatred she saw in his eyes.

''What did *I* get?'' he demanded.

''A lot of people didn't even get to come home,'' she said angrily. ''My father lost his leg in that war.''

''Losing his leg only made everyone love him all the more.'' Billy Bob sneered. ''If they only knew. I could tell you stories about your daddy and what happened over there, little girl, that would blow you out of the water. Yeah, I could.''

''I can't believe you'd pass up a ransom just for a little revenge,'' she said, suspicious that there must be more to this.

Just as she'd hoped, Billy Bob lost his cool. ''A little revenge? This is about making history. About making sure that James Marshall McCord never becomes president.''

She stared at him. ''What do you care if my father

becomes president? What possible difference could it make to you?''

''He has no right to be president,'' Billy Bob snarled. ''No right at all. I know about them politicians. Like I don't know the government's controlling the weather. All those floods and hurricanes and tornadoes. I know a lot more than they think I know. I know about all those weapons they're storing up, all the tanks and the aircrafts. McCord's in on it. You bet he is.'' Billy Bob shook his head as if lost in his own thoughts. But the pistol never wavered from her chest.

Levi exchanged a look with Seth. The man was a lunatic.

''You don't know the senator as well as you think you do,'' Seth said, obviously still hoping he could reason with him. ''You kill his daughter to try to keep him from running for president and nothing on earth will keep him out of the White House then.''

Billy Bob smiled. ''Oh, we'll see about that. Your daddy ain't going to be president. You mark my words on that, little girl.''

It was worse than Levi had thought. Billy Bob Larson was one of those wackos predicting the end of the world with the new millennium, a new world order, antigovernment extremism and conspiracy theories.

''Killing me isn't going to bring down the government,'' she said. ''Only a fool would think that.''

Billy Bob glared at her. ''You'll find out how big a fool I am.''

''I know Alex couldn't care less if the government controls the weather or the local brewery. So where does he fit in?'' Seth asked, drawing Billy Bob's attention back to him.

She saw that Seth was trying to distract him and shut her up. He'd found two ways now to shut her up.

Billy Bob just smiled then cocked a brow at Levi. ''Alex's interests were of a more *personal* nature.''

''What is he talking about?'' Levi asked, seeing the way Seth narrowed his gaze at Billy Bob.

''Nothing,'' Seth said. ''He obviously doesn't know what he's talking about.''

''The hell you say,'' Billy Bob shot back with a grin. ''First time I saw that photograph Alex kept on his cell wall at the prison, I knew he'd be of use to me.''

''What photo?'' she asked. From the expression on Seth's face he seemed to know already. She watched him rub his forehead, his gaze on the floor.

''Let me guess,'' Seth said, looking up at Billy Bob. ''You used to work as a guard at the prison.''

''What photograph?'' she asked again, feeling sick.

''Why, the one that looked just like you, Miss McCord,'' Billy Bob said. ''First time I saw that picture, I thought it *was* you. Turns out it's a woman named Shanna.''

Shanna. Levi felt her heart drop like a rock. She took a breath, her pulse roaring in her ears. ''He had a photograph in his cell of the woman he'd killed?''

''An eight-by-ten.'' The deputy shifted his gaze to Seth. ''Alex got pretty excited when I told him I knew a woman who was the spitting image of Shanna. A senator's daughter, no less. Soon to be a president's daughter if we didn't stop it.''

Billy Bob thought Shanna looked like her? Levi felt her head spin. This couldn't be.

"Alex wouldn't have been interested in your political views," Seth said. His voice sounded strange to her ears.

"You *know* what he was interested in, Gantry," Billy Bob spat out. "The same thing you're interested in."

Levi felt the deputy's lecherous gaze on her. She looked to Seth for an explanation, but he was glaring at Billy Bob. If looks could kill— My God, could it be true that she resembled Shanna?

She swallowed and took a breath. "I've seen a picture of Shanna. She doesn't look anything like me."

Billy Bob chuckled. "Oh, yeah?" He reached inside his uniform and pulled out an eight-by-ten photograph. It had been folded hastily, the corners not matching up. He handed it to her. "You be the judge."

She wondered where he'd gotten the photo as she smoothed out the creases. Was this the one that Alex had had in his prison cell? Why did Billy Bob have it? Then none of that mattered. Nothing mattered. She stared down at the woman in the picture. A more recent photo of Shanna. Only a blind fool couldn't have seen the resemblance.

Her gaze shot up to Seth. This time he didn't turn away and what she saw in his dark eyes confirmed it. He'd seen the resemblance. He knew how much she looked like Shanna. He'd known all along.

"You saw the resemblance, didn't you?" she said. "But you kept it from me. Why?"

He shook his head. "It isn't what you think."

She closed her eyes, feeling the tears dam behind them. Last night in the barn, how much of their lovemaking had been for her—and how much of it had been because she looked like Shanna?

Levi didn't remember jumping to her feet. Didn't remember swinging at Seth as he stumbled to his feet and reached for her. Crumpling the photograph of Shanna in her hands, she threw it down at Seth's feet. She was so blinded by hurt and anger, nothing mattered. Not Billy Bob and his politics or his greed or the gun in his hand. Not anything but getting out of the trailer. Getting away from Seth. Away from the shame. Shame because she'd fallen desperately in love with him and all the while his only interest in her was that she resembled a dead woman. A woman he'd once loved and obviously still did.

She could hear Billy Bob yelling for both of them to sit down and shut up. She shoved Seth, propelling him into the deputy, as she dived for the trailer door.

Behind her she heard something heavy fall and a thunder of shouts and curses. But by then she was out the door, banging past the makeshift plywood porch door, running. Running blinded by tears and pain. Just running.

THE DAMN PHOTOGRAPH! Seth cursed himself for not telling Levi the truth as he'd stepped between her and Billy Bob and the pistol. Let the deputy shoot him in the back. He didn't care. Only Levi mattered.

God, how he wanted the chance to explain his feelings to her. But he knew there was nothing he could have said. Not now. Even if Levi had stayed around to listen.

She'd shoved him as she leaped for the trailer door, throwing him off balance. He'd fallen back, his body crashing into Billy Bob's. If Billy Bob hadn't grabbed him, they both wouldn't have gone down. But they did, crashing on a heap of Delbert's junk.

After the initial shock, Billy Bob cursed as he shoved him off.

Seth got to his feet first. Unfortunately, Billy Bob hadn't dropped the gun in his fall. He knelt, the pistol in the palm of one hand, cocked and ready to shoot.

"You so much as sneeze and I'll blow you to kingdom come," Billy Bob breathed.

Seth raised his hands slowly, the crumpled photograph of Shanna in his hand from where he'd picked it up off the floor. Unconsciously, he crushed Shanna's photo in his fist. *Run, Levi, run.* He'd left the keys in the Blazer. If she could reach it before—

"She's not going to get away," Billy Bob said as if reading his mind. He gave Seth a smug grin as he got to his feet. "All of that was for nothin'. She won't make the highway."

Alex. No! She'd have escaped Billy Bob only to be caught by Alex. Seth couldn't speak. Could barely breathe. He hadn't come this far to let Alex get his hands on Levi.

He threw the balled up photo of Shanna into the deputy's smug face. At the same time, he brought his other arm down on Billy Bob's arm, the same one that held the gun, the same one that Seth had injured in their knife fight by the river yesterday. The gun hit the floor. Billy Bob let out a howl of pain and Seth slammed his body into the man, driving him backward a step.

Billy Bob howled again as Seth brought his knee up into the man's groin and hurled him into another pile of junk. He heard Billy Bob's head connect with something solid. Deputy Larson dropped like a ton of coal to the floor.

Seth scooped up the deputy's pistol from the floor and, without looking back, dived for the trailer door. He had to get to Levi before Alex did. He couldn't lose her, not now.

LEVI RAN, BLINDED BY TEARS. Hadn't she known Seth was keeping something from her?

She slipped and fell on the sun-glazed ice and lay there for a moment, too stunned, too hurt and too tired to get up. No, dammit, she hadn't known. She'd believed that when he'd made love to her he was seeing *her*. Not Shanna. Had his attraction to her only been because of Shanna?

A sound back at the trailer brought her to her feet again. The pain in her hip and butt where she'd fallen were nothing compared to the pain in her heart. She could see the Blazer parked by the road. Not that much farther.

She ran again, closing the distance between her and the car. Seth had left the keys in it, hadn't he? Suddenly she felt the hair on her neck prickle. A chill swept through her and yet the wind had died. The silence seemed as deep as the melting snowdrifts and just as cold.

She turned to look back as she reached the driver's side of the car. No one was behind her. Not even the dogs had followed her. She jumped in and started the engine, popping the clutch as she roared back onto the gravel road, not sure where it headed.

A sliver of fear wedged itself in her heart. No matter what Seth had done to her, she didn't want to leave him with Billy Bob. Not even to drive to the nearest phone for help. But going back without a weapon, without a plan, would be suicide. Not just for her but for Seth.

She had to get to a phone. Get help. But right now—

Levi wasn't sure what made her glance in the rearview mirror. A sound? Or just a feeling? She screamed as a face appeared in the mirror.

"Oh, God, it's you!" she cried.

Chapter Fourteen

Seth stumbled out of the trailer and over to the rise in the hillside to look down at the road. The Blazer was gone. Levi had gotten away. He breathed a sigh of relief. Behind him, he heard nothing, but he couldn't count on Billy Bob staying down long. He ran toward one of the school buses, needing immediate cover and time to think.

Where to now? He wished he knew what Levi would do. But the woman was unpredictable as hell. Right now she might be on her way to the airport to book a flight to Texas. *Adios, amigo.* Or...in his heart, he believed no matter how angry, upset and hurt she was with him, she wouldn't just desert him. She'd come back for him armed with nothing short of the entire cavalry.

Unless Alex had somehow gotten her. The thought burrowed deep and refused to let go. If she'd gotten away, she wouldn't come back to the trailer alone. She was too smart for that. But if Alex had her—

Seth swore and looked around. He had to get moving. A memory pulled at him. Earlier, just before he'd found Delbert's body, just before Billy

Bob had shown up in the trailer, he'd heard the whine of a snowmobile that seemed to have been headed this way. About the time the sound stopped, Billy Bob had appeared.

It was too much of a coincidence for the snowmobile not to be Billy Bob's. So where had he left it?

Seth glanced around the end of the bus and could see a stand of pines not far to the west in the direction of the main highway. Logic told him the deputy would have come from the main highway. The trees were the perfect place to hide the snowmobile.

Running across the open space between the last junk car and the pines, he ducked from one wrecked vehicle to the next until he reached the trees. Just over the rise, he saw the snowmobile.

Seth ran to it, started it up and followed the tracks to the main highway and the dark green Dodge truck backed up into a snowdrift. Seth hoped his luck was changing as he looked in to see the keys in the ignition and the gas gauge reading full.

"YOU SCARED ME half to death," Levi cried, almost driving into the ditch before she got the Blazer under control again on the narrow, hilly gravel road. "We have to help Seth!"

"Tell me where he is." Seth's partner Jerilyn climbed over the seat to join Levi in the front of the Blazer.

"Back at the trailer up on the hill," Levi said, her voice breaking. She glanced back, but the Bergstrom place had disappeared several dips in the road ago. She slowed the car, her hands trembling on the wheel and her heart still racing. She hadn't admitted to herself until that moment how afraid she'd been. Or how alone. "I'm so glad to see you. A man named Billy Bob Larson has Seth and I'm afraid—"

"The Vietnam vet and former guard from Montana State Prison," Jerilyn interrupted. "Turn around at that wide spot up ahead."

"You know about Billy Bob?" Levi asked in surprise.

"When Seth called me about Alex, I did some checking and Billy Bob's name came up," she said. "Turn around here."

"We're going back for Seth?" Levi asked as she turned the Blazer around and started back up the road. She felt such a wave of relief. Like Seth, his partner was trained for this sort of thing, right? Levi was no longer alone, no longer feeling helpless.

"Oh yeah, we're going back for Seth," Jerilyn said with conviction. "Where were you headed?"

"The cops."

Jerilyn shook her head. "Bad idea. Who knows how many other law enforcement people might be involved with Billy Bob."

"Thank God, you arrived when you did," Levi said, her gaze on the road ahead. The sun had dropped behind the mountains, leaving dusk to settle in the hollows. She'd driven at least a mile down the road. As she came up over a rise, she caught sight of one of the old buses. A little farther, she saw the trailer. Dark low smudges appeared in the hills between the trailer and the road, but nothing else. No Seth. No Billy Bob.

"The trailer's up there," she told Jerilyn as they dropped down another dip in the road. "You can't see it from here, but it's blue and white."

"I'll find it," Jerilyn said. "Pull over. I don't want Billy Bob to be able to see the Blazer from the trailer."

Levi glanced around for a place to pull off and noticed for the first time that there were no other cars in sight. "Where's your car?" she asked, not questioning until that moment how Jerilyn had ended up in the back of the Blazer.

"Stop here," Jerilyn ordered.

Levi slowed the Blazer to a stop, then looked over at the redhead. "How *did* you know to come here?"

Jerilyn looked past her in the direction of the trailer. "Seth told me on the phone that he was planning to meet Bergstrom. You're sure there isn't anyone else up there besides Billy Bob and Seth?"

Levi nodded. "Delbert Bergstrom, but he's dead."

Jerilyn opened her door, her gaze finally shifting from the hillside to Levi. "Do you have a gun?" she asked.

Levi shook her head. "Billy Bob took it. You have one though, don't you?"

"Oh yeah, I have a gun, Olivia."

SETH HAD JUST STARTED to climb into the truck when he heard the shot. He spun around. The sound had come from back in the direction of the trailer. Billy Bob couldn't have come to already, could he? But who would he be shooting at? Levi?

Without another thought, Seth turned and ran back toward the trailer. He ran rather than taking the noisy snowmobile, slipping and sliding over the melting snow, the sun dying behind the mountains, afternoon shadows pooling beneath all of Delbert

Bergstrom's junk vehicles, hoping to sneak up on Billy Bob Larson.

Seth stopped running just outside the trailer to listen. No wind. No sound. Not even the dogs. Where were the dogs? The sun dropped lower in the sky, leaving the clouds pale lavender, the color of Levi's eyes when she wasn't mad. Where was Levi?

Carefully he pried open the plywood door, surprised to find someone had turned a light on inside the trailer. A band of dirty gold spilled across the floor as he slipped inside, half expecting to be met by the dogs.

Instead he was met by silence. A stale, awful silence, tinged with the distinct scent of blood. The light came from the back of the trailer, illuminating Delbert's boots.

Seth turned back to the living room, at first thinking it was empty. A shape materialized out of the darkness of one junk-filled corner. Seth jumped and stumbled back, his eyes locking on the figure in the corner.

Billy Bob Larson sat in one of the chairs, staring at him, his hands in his lap, a dark blanket wrapped around him as if he'd gotten cold waiting for Seth to return.

Seth felt fear run like ice water through his veins. The shot had just been a ruse. Billy Bob must have dug either Seth's or Levi's gun out of the pile of debris and fired that single shot, knowing Seth could come back.

His limbs threatened to liquefy as he stared at the deputy. If Billy Bob had one of the guns under that blanket...

"Billy Bob," Seth said softly, his voice cracking

but his gaze never leaving the man's shadowed face as he carefully reached inside his coat for the pistol he'd taken earlier from the deputy. He jerked it free of the holster and, heart pounding, leveled the gun at the deputy. "Where is Levi?" he demanded. "Tell me, you son of a—"

He kicked at a pile of junk near the deputy. It toppled over, hitting the chair and Billy Bob. Billy Bob toppled too, tumbling headfirst to the floor. That's when Seth saw where the bullet had come out of Billy Bob's back. He'd been shot through the heart. Then someone had propped him up in the chair and covered him with a blanket.

Stumbling back, Seth stared down at the deputy, his heart pounding, his mouth dry. Who'd killed him? Levi? Had she come back, found one of the guns and shot Billy Bob? Seth couldn't see her shooting the man, let alone propping him up in the chair. But he could imagine Alex doing it for some sick reason.

Seth stood for a long moment, wrestling with his thoughts. Nothing made any sense. Delbert dead. Billy Bob dead. Levi missing. Seth took that back. Just knowing Alex was out there gave it all a sick kind of sense. But what frightened him more than anything was the killing. Alex was leaving dead bodies in his wake like a man who had nothing to lose. And now he might have Levi.

That's when Seth knew where he had to go. If there was any chance that Alex had Levi, Seth thought he knew where Alex would take her. Hadn't he known all along where this would end? Wasn't that the way Alex had no doubt planned it from day one? This was about revenge. Retribution. And Seth feared in his heart that he was going to have to relive Shanna's death before it would be over.

THE DRIVE TO LIVINGSTON was little more than a blur. Seth pulled up at his destination, adrenaline pumping.

Alex's home before he'd been sent to prison was a remodeled railroad car, a popular use for the old cars, especially for fishermen along the river.

Alex's overlooked the Yellowstone River on the east end of town. Seth wondered if Alex still owned it and how he'd hung on to it during his stint at Montana State Prison if that was the case. Someone on the outside would have had to pay the taxes on it. Billy Bob Larson? He wondered how long they'd been partners in crime.

Seth got out of the pickup and walked to the entrance of the railroad car. He didn't expect the door to be locked and wasn't disappointed. Alex had left it unlocked for him. The door creaked open at his push and Seth was hit with that horrible feeling of déjà vu again. The night he and Wally had found Shanna here, murdered, flickered in his mind like an old black-and-white film.

He reached for a light switch but wasn't surprised to find the electricity not hooked up. Fortunately, Billy Bob Larson's truck came equipped with a large Sheriff's Department flashlight. He flicked on the flashlight and shone it into the railroad car.

For a moment, he stood motionless, breathing hard, fighting the terror and the torture, unable to blot out the last time he'd come here.

Not again. Not again, he prayed. *Not Levi.*

Just the thought pushed him deeper into the railroad car. He stopped in the living room, terrified that history was about to repeat itself.

The fact that the place looked exactly as it had eight years ago added to that déjà vu feeling. It was as if time had stood still. Even the calendar on the wall was the same.

Seth shone the flashlight down the narrow dark hallway, past the apartment-sized kitchen. The door to the bedroom stood slightly ajar, as it had the night he'd found Shanna. He could see a corner of the bed.

He didn't want to go down that hallway. Didn't want to remember the other time and finding Shanna lying murdered on that bed, a bullet through her heart. But more than anything, he didn't want the same thing to have happened to Levi. No, not Levi.

He told himself he was wrong. Levi wasn't here. Had never been here. This time his gut instinct was way off base. He was just living his worst nightmare, that's all. There was nothing for him here. So why did he insist on putting himself through this again?

He stood for a moment, staring down the hallway at the partially closed bedroom door, trying desperately to exorcise the memory of Shanna's body on that bed. He knew he couldn't turn around and leave. Not yet. He had to know. Something had made him come here.

He started toward the bedroom door, unable to stop himself as badly as he wished he could. But he hadn't gotten two feet when he stumbled in midstep. A flash of color caught his eye. He swung his gaze to it. His heart stopped.

Curled on the tiny patch of linoleum kitchen floor was a thin strand of pale lavender.

Fighting for his next breath, he slowly knelt down and picked up the ribbon, the satin cool against his fingers. It was the ribbon he'd untied from Levi's hair last night before he'd made love with her. The same ribbon he'd watched her tie into her braid this morning.

He brought the fabric to his face, cupping it over his nose and mouth, breathing in the scent of her, and squeezed his eyes closed. Levi. His heart cried out her name over and over. Levi.

She'd been here. He balled the ribbon in his fist and opened his eyes. She could still be here.

He rushed down the hallway and slammed the bedroom door open, unable to stand it any longer. "Levi!" he cried, his gaze flying to the bed and the pale lavender of Levi's dress on the bedcovers.

"Levi!" Seth reached for her, his hands coming up with only the pale lavender fabric in his fingers. He stared at it and then the bed, too stunned at first to comprehend.

He'd expected to see Levi there—just as he'd found Shanna. It took him a moment to realize there was no body on the bed—only Levi's dress.

He stood trembling, the dress in his hands, relief and fear running tandem through his veins, making him weak and scared and crazy. Where now? But he already knew.

He started for the door, desperately wanting out of this place. But just as he was leaving the railroad car, something caught his eye. He stopped and stared down at the calendar that had fallen to the floor. A strangely familiar face looked up at him from the family photograph on the top half of the calendar.

Seth picked up the 1975 calendar from the floor and saw that there was writing on it. "Alex, I marked all our special days, Love always, Jolene" had been scrawled across the month of January. The calendar was compliments of Robson Cleaners of Billings. Robson Cleaners. The two words Levi had found written and circled on Wally's scratch pad.

Seth studied the girl in the family picture, wondering why she looked so familiar. Her face had been circled in red pen in the shape of a heart. He glanced down at the names under each snapshot. The little girl with the small brown eyes and the blunt-cut mousy brown hair and the buck teeth was Jolene Robson, age eight. Cut the hair, dye it, straighten the teeth, add two dozen years to her age and you had—

No, it couldn't be! He studied the little girl's eyes. Wasn't that what had made him notice her photo in the first place? Weren't the eyes what had looked so familiar when everything else about Jolene Robson had changed over the years. But not the eyes. The eyes were the same.

Seth swore. Jolene Robson was Jerilyn Ryers! His partner in his security business in Austin. Alex Wells's girlfriend from Billings. The one Shanna had found out about eight years ago.

Chapter Fifteen

Levi woke to darkness and cold and a terrible throbbing in her head. It took her a moment to realize that her wrists and ankles were bound. She lifted her head and dropped it again to keep from blacking out. *Slowly,* she told herself. *Move slowly.* It was all she could do to listen, though. Panic and pain had her body in overdrive, frizzing out her brain with screaming white light.

Settle down. You're alive. It was the only good thing she could think of. She lifted her head again, slowly, carefully. She was in the back seat of the Blazer. Darkness had closed in around it and as far as she could tell, she was alone, parked somewhere.

She laid her head back on the seat and closed her eyes, trying to get her bearings. Her thoughts raced past at warp speed, one memory coming into focus. That terrifying moment when she'd looked into the rearview mirror and seen Jerilyn Ryers.

Jerilyn was the last person she'd expected to see. Levi had recognized her instantly as the redhead in the middle of the road on Thanksgiving Day. The woman who'd laid down her bike and her life for Seth. Seth's partner.

Jerilyn had come to help her. Well, maybe not her. But Seth anyway. Why couldn't Levi remember what had happened after that?

She heard the sound of footfalls outside the Blazer. A door opened and someone slid into the front seat. She could hear muttering and smell the smoke of a cigarette coming from the front seat.

She listened and realized the voice she heard was Jerilyn's. Who was she talking to? Seth? Levi pushed herself up, the nausea making her sick, but she finally got herself wedged in the corner against the door and seat so she was upright and facing the front.

Jerilyn was alone in the front seat, bent over the wheel as she started the Blazer and muttered to herself. She took a long drag on her cigarette once she got the engine going and turned to look behind her, seemingly startled to see Levi.

"So you're awake," she said as she backed the Blazer up, then shifted into first and turned her attention to the narrow, rutted dirt road in the headlights.

"What happened?" Levi asked, fear, pain and confusion giving her a blinding headache.

Jerilyn darted a look in the rearview mirror, then swore and swerved to keep the Blazer on the road.

The eyes that met Levi's were hard and cold with anger. But it was the vacant look in them that froze Levi's blood. They were the eyes of a person who'd gone completely insane.

"What are you looking at?" Jerilyn snapped. She was driving slowly, the road rough.

Levi shook her head and swallowed hard, her mouth cotton dry, her head a dull ache, her body weak as water. "Can you untie my hands? The cord is cutting off my circulation."

Fury fired the redhead's brown eyes. "Isn't that just too bad. You always were such a whiner, Shanna. Whiny and wimpy. I'll never understand what Alex sees in you."

Levi stared at the woman, her heart pounding, her pulse a roar in her ears. "I'm not Shanna. I'm Levi McCord."

Jerilyn smiled. "And I'm not Jerilyn Ryers. My name is Jolene Robson." She laughed. "But you and I know the truth. We know who we really are, don't we?"

Robson. Where had Levi heard that name before?

Levi frantically looked around the back of the Blazer for something to cut the cord on her hands. She discovered a metal ice scraper on the floorboards. Trapping it between her boots, she twisted to one side and lifted it up to her hands when Jerilyn wasn't watching.

Levi wasn't sure she had enough time before Jerilyn stopped the car again, but she had to try to get loose. She got the scraper behind her and began working at the cord. "Where are we going?"

Jerilyn, or was her name really Jolene Robson, shot her a sly look. "As if you didn't know."

Levi had no idea. But she had a feeling Shanna would have known. "You knew Shanna?" she asked, hoping Jerilyn would realize she had the wrong woman.

Jerilyn laughed, the laugh of a person who's dropped over the edge. "Knew Shanna? Oh, I knew her all right. She tried to take Alex from me. Stupid woman. I knew it wouldn't last but I didn't feel like waiting. I wanted her out of our lives. For good. I never wanted to see her face again. I wanted her dead.''

Levi let out a strangled cry and almost dropped the scraper. "*You* killed her?"

Jerilyn smiled back in the rearview mirror. "The sniveling little bitch deserved it. Killing her seemed the best way to make sure she didn't come back. Ever.''

Levi stared at the woman.

Jerilyn threw on the brakes, almost sending Levi tumbling to the floorboards. "But then Shanna came back, didn't she?''

The woman's eyes locked with hers. Levi felt her blood solidify. She stared at the redhead, her heart pounding so loudly it was all she could hear in the confines of the Blazer as a thought zipped past. Hadn't Seth said Shanna found out about a girlfriend in Billings? Wasn't that why Shanna had gone out to Alex's that night? "*You* were the girlfriend from Billings.''

"You, of all people, should know that." Her eyes narrowed. "So why am I looking into your face again?''

"Because I'm not Shanna, I'm Levi. Levi McCord, remember?''

Jerilyn blinked and looked back at the road. She started the Blazer moving again. "Levi. Seth's Levi." She lit another cigarette. Levi noticed that the woman's hands were trembling.

"Where is Seth?" Levi asked as she got a clear memory of Jerilyn planning to go up to the trailer just before...just before the woman had knocked her out.

"That no-account deputy let him get away," Jerilyn snapped. "If he'd just killed the two of you like
I told him to—"

Seth got away? Levi felt relief wash over her. She
tried to clear the dullness from her brain, knowing
it was her only hope. Jerilyn had told Billy Bob to
kill them?

Why hadn't Jerilyn killed her when she'd had the
chance back there? Why tie her up? And where was
she taking her now? The woman obviously thought
she was Shanna. So why had she spared her this
time? And where was Seth? Would he know where
she'd gone? Would he come looking for her? Or was
that exactly what Jerilyn was hoping?

The wind rocked the Blazer and dirt pelted the
windows like rain. They had to be near Livingston.
Levi tried the door at her side, planning to throw
herself out and take her chances once they got close
enough to town. But the door had been child-proof
locked from up front.

"It's better this way," Jerilyn was saying.
"Meant to be, I guess. This time you'll die in front
of Alex."

Jerilyn planned to kill her in front of Alex? The
woman *was* insane. Levi felt panic race through her
as hot and fast as wildfire. She had to get out of the
Blazer. Had to escape. She worked frantically at the
cord but realized she had to keep Jerilyn talking.
Talking and driving, keep her busy. All Levi needed
was a few more minutes.

"I thought you loved Alex," she said, trying to
keep the panic out of her voice. The cord on her
wrists began to fray under the pressure of the

scraper. "How could you let him go to prison for a murder he didn't commit, if you loved him?"

"I loved him but he had to pay for what he'd done," Jerilyn said calmly, logically. "He hurt me. He had to go to prison to pay for what he'd done to me. Then, if he proved himself worthy, I had a surprise for him. Eleven million dollars."

That number rang a bell even in Levi's aching head. The armored car robbery. "You robbed the armored car and set up Seth!" Levi tried to get her trembling fingers to work faster.

Jerilyn didn't seem to hear her. "I waited for Alex. I thought there was still a chance for us once he got out of prison. I would have given him anything. I even planned to frame Seth for Shanna's murder, vindicating Alex. We would have been rich and free." Her gaze flicked to the mirror again. "But then you came back."

"I'm not Shanna, remember?"

"I wonder where that damned Seth is," Jerilyn muttered as she slowed the Blazer and turned.

The road got jarringly rougher. Levi thought she could make out a large odd-shaped building ahead. The abandoned railroad roundhouse on the east end of town?

"I don't understand why you and Alex don't take off with the robbery money," Levi said. The cord was frayed and thin. Just a little more. "Why stay here and take the chance of getting caught by killing more people when you are finally free to be with the man you love? It's not too late."

Oh, how Levi ached to be with the man she loved. She prayed Seth was all right. The cord thinned until it finally snapped. She kept her hands behind her, biding her time, as hard as it was to wait.

Jerilyn brought the Blazer to a stop. Outside, a brick building loomed up out of the darkness.

"Why? Because of *you*," Jerilyn said, her gaze fired with hatred as it glared back at Levi from the mirror. "Haven't you figured it out by now?"

Levi didn't move. Not a muscle.

"I knew the minute I laid eyes on you," Jerilyn said. "Alex had lied to me. He was still in love with you."

"With Shanna?"

"Why else did he get involved with Billy Bob after he said he wanted to go straight?"

Jerilyn turned off the engine, glared at the building in front of them and took a long drag on her cigarette. She blew smoke at the mirror as she looked back at Levi again. "I wondered why Alex would get mixed up with some antigovernment wacko. It wasn't like him. But then I saw you—"

Levi thought about the first time she'd seen the redhead in the middle of the road on Thanksgiving Day. The memory flickered before her, foggy at first, then clearer. The redhead getting to her feet and turning. Jerilyn's surprised expression. It hadn't made any sense then. Nor had Levi remembered it until now. Jerilyn had seen the resemblance between Levi and Shanna, that's why she'd looked so surprised.

"I knew then why Alex got involved," Jerilyn spat. "He's never gotten over you. That's why I have to kill you. Again. Kill you in front of Alex and Seth when he shows up. Seth will know where to find you."

"How could Seth? He has no idea where I am," Levi said, not sure that was true.

Jerilyn laughed. "You underestimate Seth. I know the man." She smiled, making Levi sick inside. "He'll be here. He'll follow the same path he did when he went looking for Shanna and it will lead him right to you. Right to me. Right to his destiny."

Oh, my God, Levi thought. If Jerilyn was right, Seth would be walking into a trap.

"Then I'll have to stop by the hospital on my way out of town and take care of Wally," Jerilyn was saying. "No loose ends. I wonder what the weather is like in South America this time of year. Warm, don't you think?"

Jerilyn opened the car door and got out and walked around to the door nearest Levi. Levi knew she had to find some way to stop the woman before they went inside the building. God only knows what awaited her inside. Hadn't the chef at Chico said Alex had been missing for two days?

Jerilyn jerked open the door and, brandishing a pistol, ordered, "Get out."

"That could be a little difficult," Levi said, motioning to her bound ankles.

"Oh, you always were such a pansy, Shanna," Jerilyn spat. "So helpless." Jerilyn cursed as she reached down to untie the cord with her free hand, the pistol pointed at the ground in the other hand.

Levi waited until Jerilyn was almost finished before she made her move. She brought her hands down hard on the nape of Jerilyn's neck in an ad-libbed karate chop. At the same time, she brought her knees up into the redhead's face.

Jerilyn let out a cry and fell backward to the

ground. Levi clambered from the Blazer, her gaze frantically searching for the gun. It lay next to Jerilyn, who was now holding her bleeding nose with both hands.

Levi dived for the gun.

SETH THREW DOWN the calendar and bolted out through the railroad car door to the truck. In the distance, the locomotive roundhouse hunkered dark black against the night sky. That was where he'd find Levi. The same place he'd find Jolene and Alex. His gut instinct told him so.

In the truck, he pulled down Billy Bob's shotgun but soon threw it aside when he realized the deputy had taken all the shells. All he had was the pistol he'd taken from Billy Bob. It would have to suffice.

As he drove away from Alex's railroad car, Seth glanced back, all the anguished memories of Shanna following him, just as he knew they would. Could he ever get away from them? Would he ever be free?

He looked to the road ahead. He drove faster, as if through speed alone he could outrun the past. He wanted to be free of Shanna. He was going after Levi. His heart told him she was still alive. Jolene wouldn't kill her—not until he got there.

He told himself he'd get another chance. To love again. To love Levi, free and clear of the past. But he couldn't go another day without telling her that he loved her because, dammit, he *did* love her. And the past be damned, he wanted her—not some image of Shanna he found in her.

But first he had to get Levi away from Alex and Jolene. *Then* he could try to make her understand.

As he drove toward the railroad building, he wondered which would be harder to do.

THE CORD HAD CUT OFF some of the circulation to Levi's legs, but she hadn't realized it until it was too late. She dived for the gun, but her ankles were weak. She stumbled, falling.

Jolene moved more quickly. Spurred by anger and insanity and a need for the deadliest of revenge, she got to the gun first and, after picking it up, swung it at Levi.

The blow glanced off Levi's shoulder but still knocked her to the ground. Jolene grabbed a handful of Levi's hair and jerked her to her feet, ramming the pistol into her side. Jolene half dragged her over to the building and shoved her up against the wall.

"You look like her, but you don't act like her," the redhead said, eyeing Levi suspiciously. "Either that or you've gotten tougher. Maybe death does that to you."

"I'm not dead." At least not yet.

Jolene dragged her over the railroad track to the door of the building. Levi watched as the redhead dug out a key for the large padlock. When the door fell open, Jolene pushed her inside.

Levi stumbled into the darkness to fall over something large and soft on the floor and land on the cold concrete floor. A moan echoed through the eerie, empty silence of the building.

"I see you've found Alex," Jolene said with a laugh.

Levi jerked away from the body in the dark. Behind her she heard the scratch of a match. Light flickered, exposing a small circle of the cavernous insides of the building.

Jolene lit another candle. Then another. But the faint lights did little to chase away the cold or the dark.

At least now, Levi could see the man on the floor beside her. Alex. He would have looked like the photograph she'd seen of him except for the huge dark bruise around his left eye and the discolored bump on his forehead.

Jolene kicked at the man bound on the floor beside Levi.

"Wake him up," she ordered, handing Levi a water bottle. "I want him conscious for this."

Levi did as she was told, squirting water in his face.

Alex Wells stirred. His blue eyes opened, then blinked. He jerked back as if he'd seen a ghost. A sharp cry escaped his lips.

Jolene let out a satisfied chuckle, then a curse. "I brought your precious Shanna to you, Alex. What do you say?"

His eyes studied her face closely. Levi saw him realize that she wasn't Shanna, nor was she a ghost.

"I'm Levi McCord," she said quietly.

He nodded. "The resemblance is startling."

"So I've heard," Levi said. And *seen* with her own eyes. But she didn't want to mention the photograph. She and Alex were in enough trouble without that.

"Untie him," Jolene ordered.

Levi did as she was told, fear a hard, cold knot in her stomach.

"Jolene," Alex said as he sat up, rubbing his

wrists, then his ankles. "We both know this isn't Shanna."

"Isn't it, Alex?" Jolene asked sweetly. "Isn't she the reason you went along with Billy Bob's hare-brained plan?"

"No, Jolene, it isn't," he said as he got to his feet. Levi did the same, drawing Alex's gaze. He seemed at a loss as to what to say to the redhead. "I didn't want to see Olivia McCord killed. That's why I pretended to be on Billy Bob's side."

Jolene smiled. "You lied to me, Alex. I thought you really were helping Billy Bob and all the time you just didn't want to see your precious Shanna killed again."

He shook his head, but Levi could see that it hurt him to do so. "I just don't want any more killing."

"Too bad," Jolene said. "Dammit, Seth, where are you?" she yelled. Her words echoed through the building.

Alex looked at Levi with the same question. She shrugged. She wished she knew. There was nothing she wanted to see more than his handsome face. But not here. Not now.

Levi glanced into the darkness, looking for a weapon, something to distract Jolene and give them a chance to overpower her. The cavernous building had little to offer. She could see a maze of narrow walkways overhead. They ran across the high ceiling in a web that matched the dark gaping holes like grease pits on the floor and the railroad tracks that ran parallel to them where the locomotives had once been worked on.

She realized that had she stumbled past Alex's body on the floor, she would have fallen headlong into one of those deep, dark pits. Is that what had happened to Wally?

Was this where Seth had cornered Alex before the cops arrived? Where their friendship had ended, both of them blaming the other for Shanna's death when it had been Jolene all along?

And was this where it would end permanently for her and Seth and Alex? She wondered how long it would take for someone to find their bodies in here. The thought made her shudder.

"I guess it doesn't matter if Seth makes it or not," Jolene said, more to herself than to Levi or Alex. "I'll find him and take care of him."

Levi caught a movement out of the corner of her eye. At first she thought she'd only imagined it. In the darkness, something moved. A shape. Large, man-size. Then she saw him. Seth. He motioned for her to remain silent as he started down one of the walkways that crossed directly over their heads.

For once, Levi did as he asked. Not that she could have spoken for the life of her. She swallowed, her mouth dry as dust, and glanced over at Alex. His gaze acknowledged that he too had seen Seth.

"Time's up," Jolene said. "We can't wait any longer."

"Jolene, don't do this," Alex pleaded. "It accomplishes nothing."

"You don't understand, Alex. I'm going to keep killing Shanna, again and again." Suddenly the laugh turned into crying. "I'm going to keep killing her and keep killing her until—" She choked on a sob.

"Until what, Jolene?" Alex asked softly.

"Until I kill your love for her," the redhead an-

swered. One moment she sounded like a child, another moment a woman scorned and insane. What a
combination. She dried her tears with the back of
her hand and cocked the pistol and leveled it at
Levi's heart.

Levi could feel Alex's fear that Seth wouldn't be
able to get to them in time and Levi didn't think
reasoning with Jolene was going to save them.

"I want to help you, Jolene," Alex said.

"Help me?" She laughed. "I worked my way
into Seth Gantry's life, into his business, into his
trust. I robbed an armored car single-handedly and
framed him for it. I foiled Seth's plans and have the
woman he tried so hard to protect. You both tried
so hard to protect," she added. "And you want to
help *me?*"

"Give me the gun," Alex said as he put himself
between Levi, and Jolene and the gun.

"Alex, oh, Alex," she said in a singsong voice.
"There is nothing you can do to keep me from killing your sweet Shanna."

A gunshot echoed through the building.

"That was just a warning shot," Jolene said, and
took aim again. "This one is for real."

The revolver boomed. Alex dropped at Levi's
feet.

"DAMMIT, JOLENE!" Alex cried. Blood poured
from his thigh, but Levi could see that Jolene had
only wounded him. Any question Levi had about
Jolene's shooting abilities were instantly put to rest.

Levi glanced up and saw Seth directly overhead.
Her eyes widened as she saw what he planned to
do. Jump! If he missed, he'd end up in the pit.

"Goodbye, Shanna," Jolene said, then must have realized that Levi's attention was elsewhere. As Jolene started to swing her gaze and the gun toward the ceiling and Seth, Levi leaped at her. Another shot thundered through the building. Levi's momentum sent both her and Jolene to the floor. Levi heard the gun skitter across the concrete and past the circle of light into the blackness.

Jolene immediately crawled after the pistol. Levi clutched at her, grabbing her leg, but Jolene kicked free and lunged for the gun.

Seth hit the floor with a thud, rolled and cursed. Something metal clattered to the floor. Levi turned in time to see Seth grab his left arm in pain. Just out of his reach, she saw the gun that he'd dropped after his painful jump.

But before Levi could move, Jolene swung around, the revolver again in her hand. She pointed it at Levi's head and smiled.

Seth shoved Levi out of the way and leaped at Jolene just an instant before she pulled the trigger. The shot went wild.

Levi watched in horror as Jolene and Seth struggled for the pistol, Seth able to use only his right arm to battle her. His left arm dangled uselessly at his side. Alex had gotten to his feet and was headed over to help Seth.

The other gun. *Get the other gun!* Levi scrambled for the gun that Seth had dropped. She heard another shot echo through the building and looked back to see that Jolene had shot Alex again. This time he lay on the floor, unmoving, his left shoulder soaked with blood.

Seth's gun. Levi grabbed it and swung around.

Seth had Jolene against the wall of the building, but she still had the gun and they were still struggling.

Levi leveled the gun at Jolene, trying to get a clean shot.

"Shoot!" Seth cried.

She could hear the pain in his voice.

Levi felt the pistol begin to shake in her hands. She couldn't. She couldn't shoot. Not with Seth so close.

Jolene struck Seth's broken arm, doubling him over and driving him back. It all happened in an instant. Jolene looked up to see Levi with the gun leveled at her chest. The redhead lowered her revolver, smiled and shook her head. She knew Levi couldn't shoot her.

If Jolene had even looked as though she might turn her gun on Seth, Levi told herself she would have fired. Her finger twitched, a breath of a movement on the trigger. But Jolene turned and disappeared out the door.

Levi watched her go, unable to move, hardly able to breathe. She lowered the gun and started toward Seth. But she never reached him. He stumbled after Jolene and into the night.

"Let her go," Levi cried after him. But it was too late, Seth was already gone. Then she heard it. A train whistle. The floor began to shake and a rumble seemed to move through the entire building. The train was coming! And it sounded as though it was on the tracks right outside the door.

The lights of the train exploded around her as Levi stumbled out of the building. In that flash of an instant, she saw Seth running after Jolene on the other side of the tracks toward the railroad bridge, only yards away. She saw Jolene turn to shoot at Seth.

Levi stumbled toward the tracks, her only thought getting to Seth. But the train was suddenly in front of her, a rumbling roar of moving wall, clanking cars rocking and rattling over the tracks in a deafening rumble.

She leaped back, pressing herself against the wall of the building, the train so close its wind tore at her clothing. She closed her eyes, Seth's name on her lips. But she couldn't hold the tears in. They poured down her cheeks. She should have shot Jolene when she had the chance. Now Jolene may have killed Seth and gotten away.

The train flickered beyond her closed eyelids, car after car, the rumble inside her chest as deafening as her pounding broken heart.

Then the train was gone, the last car rocking by, disappearing into the night. She opened her eyes and stood for a moment staring blindly into the darkness, expecting to see Seth lying on the other side, dead, and Jolene gone.

But she could see nothing but darkness. Then suddenly, from beside her, the headlights from the Blazer flashed on, arcing light down the tracks to the bridge that spanned the Yellowstone River.

Levi saw Jolene. She was on the railroad bridge, Seth right behind her. Jolene turned and fired behind her, the shot exploding in the dead silence after the train. Seth fell. Levi watched in horror as Jolene began to walk slowly back toward him, the revolver in her hand, a deadly smile on her face.

Levi raised the pistol still in her hand. Jolene saw

her but paid no attention. Levi fired, the report echoing off the side of the building.

Jolene looked up and for one heart-stopping moment Levi thought she'd missed. Now Jolene would fire another shot at Seth—the one that would undoubtedly kill him. If he wasn't already dead. But then she saw Jolene limping, her side darkening with blood as she moved toward Seth.

How many times had Jolene shot? Five or six? Was she out of bullets—or did she have one more shot?

Levi wasn't sure. She trained the pistol on the redhead, this time shooting to kill. Just as Levi started to fire again, Jolene dropped to her knees at the edge of the tracks, the gun aimed directly at Seth's head. She smiled and pulled the trigger. The hammer hit on an empty cylinder with a dull thunk. Then Jolene fell over, toppling off the bridge.

"Seth!" Levi ran, screaming Seth's name again and again. She stumbled to him and knelt down beside him.

Seth gazed up at her. *Thank God,* she cried inwardly. *He's still alive.* She could see the pain in his face and blood where a bullet had grazed his forehead.

"I have to tell you something," he whispered. "I love you."

Her heart lurched, and fresh tears rushed to her eyes, blinding her. "Are you—"

"I'm not saying that because I'm dying," he said, his voice a little stronger. "I'm all right, except for my arm. I think it's broken."

She helped Seth to his feet. *I love you.* The words she'd wanted desperately to hear him say. But was he saying them to her because he loved *her*—or the image of Shanna he saw in her? She wondered if she would always question that.

Levi looked up to see a dark figure silhouetted against the pickup's headlights. Alex limped to them.

''Is Jolene—'' Alex glanced over the edge of the bridge.

Below them, Jolene Robson aka Jerilyn Ryers lay broken on the rocks below, staring blankly up at the sky as if she'd been hit by a train.

Seth pulled Levi to him with his good arm and the three of them walked toward the lights of the Blazer.

Chapter Sixteen

It was late by the time the police got through taking her statement. Levi felt numb. She knew she should have felt more relief. It was over. She was safe. Seth was safe. But that was the problem: it was over.

A police officer dropped her at a motel, where she called her father. He'd wanted her to fly out that night, but she assured him she'd be home on the first flight in the morning.

Then she called the hospital to check on Seth and Alex. Alex was in stable condition with two gunshot wounds, neither life threatening, but he wouldn't be going anywhere for a while.

Seth had been treated for a broken arm and released. She wondered if he was on a small jet headed back for Texas. She wondered if she'd ever see him again.

After a hot bath, still bruised and sore and aching, she went to bed thinking she would fall into an exhausted sleep the moment her head touched the pillow. Instead she lay staring up at the ceiling reliving the past three days with Seth.

Unfortunately, it always had the same ending.

She must have slept at some point, because she

awoke to sunlight streaming through the window and someone pounding at her door.

"SETH."

That's all Levi said when she opened the door. Not exactly the greeting he'd hoped for. But he figured it was better than having the door slammed in his face. Of course, that was still an option.

"I would have knocked on your door sooner, but I figured you needed your rest," he said, his hat in his hand. "I got the room next door. Didn't sleep much though."

"Me neither." She wore a motel robe in a soft pink. It looked good on her. Real good.

"How's your arm?" she asked.

"Simple fracture," he said, holding up the casted arm. "Six weeks and it should be as good as new." He met her gaze. "Could we talk?"

She smiled at that. Not one of her spectacular ones that knocked you off your feet, but still a smile.

He smiled back hopefully. "Yeah, Seth Gantry wanting to talk, go figure." He knew it was too late to offer his life story. His only hope was to try to make her understand how he felt about her. And about Shanna. He hoped his luck had changed. He was about to find out.

She led him into the room. He'd have ordered coffee and breakfast, but he couldn't be sure he'd still be here when it arrived. The last thing he wanted to do was be presumptuous.

"I want to tell you about Shanna," he said as they sat down at the small table by the window. Sunlight poured in, golden and warm, but he felt cold and scared. Nothing had ever mattered more to him than this. He doubted anything ever would.

He took a breath. "I did love Shanna. She was a wonderful woman. She helped me through a rough time in my life and I think she made me a better person because I knew her."

"You still love her, Seth."

He saw tears well in Levi's beautiful violet eyes before she looked away. Lovingly he reached out to lift her chin with his fingers and turn her face back to him. "Yes, I suppose part of me will always love Shanna and I will always feel bad that Jolene killed her. But, Levi, you made me realize something. It wouldn't have worked with Shanna and me even had she lived."

"Because of Alex."

"No, because of me," Seth said. "I made her more like what I wanted in my mind. For eight years I remembered her the way I wanted her to be. But last night I remembered Shanna the way she really was. She was a special woman, but I always wanted her to be more—" he smiled "—more like you."

She raised a brow. "Seth, you didn't know me yet."

He chuckled. "No, not yet, but, Levi, you're what I had always wished Shanna was. Strong, determined, independent, a spitfire of a woman who would spend the rest of my life challenging me, loving me, giving me a real run for my money. Someone I considered an equal. A life partner."

"Seth—"

"Princess," he continued before she could shut him down, "I'm trying to tell you I know now that Shanna never was the woman for me. You are."

"How can I be sure, Seth?" she asked, tears brimming again in her eyes.

"I think you're already sure." He hoped his gut instinct didn't let him down. Not this time. "You're just scared. But maybe it's too soon for you. I just want you to know I love you, Levi. I've only said those words once before. Only back then, I had no idea what they meant. I do now."

She shook her head. When a tear rolled down her cheek, he reached out and thumbed it away. Desperately he wanted to take her in his arms. Well, his good arm, anyway. To make her understand, if not with words, then with his body, with his touch. But he knew making love to her would solve nothing and only make parting that much more of an agony.

"I need time, Seth. I'm not sure about anything right now."

He nodded. "Take all the time you need," he said, wondering how he would get through it, how he would survive until he saw her again. "I'll be here."

"You're staying in Montana?"

He nodded. "This is home. I hadn't realized how much I'd missed it until I came back here with you. I keep seeing you and me ranching here. Those half-dozen children, give or take three. Maybe a dog or two. A pickup truck."

"Are you serious, Seth?"

"I'm dead serious, Olivia. You're what I've been looking for my whole life." *Don't push, Gantry.* He got to his feet. "I'll be out at the Double Bar G."

It took every ounce of strength he had to walk away from her. He stepped to the door, his hat still in his hand. "Just do one thing for me. Promise me that you'll follow your heart.'' He only hoped it would lead her back to him.

LEVI WATCHED HIM GO. Her heart cried out for her to go after him. But she couldn't. Not until she could give her heart freely, without reservations or doubts.

Follow her heart? How could she trust her heart? She didn't even feel she could trust her instincts.

Her life was in Texas. The Altamira Ranch. She had responsibilities. Her father needed her. Especially now, now that he would be running for president.

She picked up the phone and dialed the airport, making reservations on the first flight to Texas. Then she called for a rental car to drive to Gallatin Field airport outside of Bozeman.

She was going home. Home. The sobs came up from deep within her and she cried, her heart breaking. But she told herself she'd made the right decision.

SETH WENT TO THE HOSPITAL first. Wally had regained consciousness late last night and Seth had spent a little time with him but they hadn't had a chance to talk. He was anxious to see Wally but first he went down the hall to Alex's room.

Alex was sitting up in the bed, surrounded by newspapers. He motioned Seth in. ''From felon to hero,'' he said, pushing the papers aside. ''It's hard to comprehend.''

Seth knew he was talking about a lot more than being a hero. ''You lost eight years of your life.''

Alex nodded. ''I didn't know Jolene was that sick.''

"No one did," he said. "She fooled us all. Especially me. Don't blame yourself for her."

Alex glanced away, but not before Seth had seen the pain in his face. "I'm sorry, Seth. Sorry about…everything."

They'd both falsely accused each other of Shanna's murder. They'd both suffered her loss. For the first time Seth realized just what losing Shanna had meant to Alex. If it was anything like Seth's feelings for Levi—

"We're both sorry, Alex."

Alex turned back to him and slowly held out his hand.

He shook Alex's hand.

"I hope…" Alex shrugged. "You know what I hope."

Seth nodded. The past was finally dead. Finally laid to rest. Maybe now they could get on with their lives. Seth knew he planned to. Whether they could be friends again remained to be seen. But Seth hoped for the same thing.

"You're a free man," he said.

"Yeah." Alex glanced toward the window. He didn't look like a free man. Nor a hero. He looked like a man with a lot of heartache. "I'll always love Shanna." Alex shifted his gaze back to Seth and smiled ruefully. "But she's gone. If she can find peace, maybe I can, too."

DOWN THE HALL, the nurse met Seth outside Wally's room.

"He's awake and kicking up a fuss to see you," she said.

Wally lay in the hospital bed, his head propped

up, his eyes open, looking so much like his old self that Seth had to smile.

"It's about time you got here," Wally said, his voice still weak. "This place is buzzing with stories. I don't know what to believe." His eyes narrowed. "You know about Jolene Robson?"

"That she was Jerilyn Ryers?"

Wally shook his head. "I was afraid you'd find out too late."

"Almost did." He held up his casted arm.

"Alex? You know he's the one who got me onto Jolene. She'd been writing him at prison. When I saw the Texas postmark on one of her letters, I just got a feeling, you know?"

Seth knew.

"Then Alex contacted me when Billy Bob Larson approached him with a plan to kill Olivia McCord. How is she?"

"Fine," Seth said, and looked away. "On her way back to Texas." Quickly he switched subjects. "Alex is a hero, you know. Jolene confessed to killing Shanna. She also was the one who'd robbed that armored car I'd been hired to protect. Alex and Levi saved my life last night."

"Jolene killed Shanna." Wally was silent for a moment. "What kind of woman would kill another woman like that?" Wally was from the old school, a generation that didn't like to believe that a woman could kill. He should have met Jolene.

"Deputy Billy Bob Larson's dead. Jolene shot him, ending their little secret partnership."

"Why?" Wally asked.

Seth knew Wally wasn't asking why Jolene shot Billy Bob. Anyone who met Billy Bob wanted to shoot him. Seth shook his head. "A woman scorned, I guess. She loved Alex. And hated him for falling for Shanna." Sometimes things just didn't make sense. Seth was glad he was a rancher and not a private investigator anymore. As a private investigator, he'd wanted to make sense of things, he'd wanted to know why, just like Wally.

"Olivia's all right?" Wally asked again. "How about you?"

"Simple fracture. Cast comes off in six weeks."

"I wasn't asking about your arm," Wally said.

Seth smiled ruefully. "I know you weren't."

"She got to you, didn't she," Wally said. "I have a feeling you got to her, too, son."

"I guess only time will tell."

When Seth left the hospital, he drove down to the cemetery, parked and walked the short distance to Shanna's grave. Wally had put up a headstone, a thick chunk of smooth granite with her name and the dates from birth to death. In smaller print, etched in the stone, were the words Rest In Peace.

Maybe Alex was right. Maybe now Shanna could. Maybe they all could.

Seth bowed his head as he knelt down in the snow beside the grave. He closed his eyes, thinking how he'd tried to let go of her but hadn't been able to, even after her death. But he could now. It was as if he'd been released from the past.

He finally understood what Shanna had been trying to tell him about love. Theirs had never been the true one, not the forever-after kind of love. And now Seth knew it, too.

He also knew Shanna would have liked Levi, and he knew she'd be happy for him. He'd not only found peace but the kind of love that made dreams come true. In his heart, he held on to the hope that Levi would be coming back. Someday soon.

He opened his eyes and smiled. "Goodbye, Shanna," he said. Then he stood and turned and walked toward the Blazer, his step lighter than it had been in eight years. He didn't look back as he got into the car and drove away. On the way to the Double Bar G, snow began to fall in large lacy flakes. He thought of Levi.

LEVI STOOD IN THE TERMINAL at Gallatin Field, staring up at the metal waterfowl that hung above the stairs to her gate. All she had to do was walk up those steps and get on the plane. The plane that would take her back to Texas. Back home. Back to her life.

Home.

At one time, no word would have sounded better. Except for those three little deadly ones Seth had uttered earlier. I love you.

She'd heard him out. Listened to his entire story. But could she believe him? Her heart already believed, but her head—

She looked up the stairs toward her gate, then at her watch. If she hurried she had time to call the ranch.

"When is your flight?" her father asked.

"In five minutes." She looked out. It was snowing huge lazy flakes that drifted down silently. "Daddy—" Her voice broke, tears filled her eyes. She found herself spilling the whole story to her father. Not about Jolene and Billy Bob and Alex. He'd already heard that one.

No, this story was about Seth Gantry.

"Levi," James Marshall McCord said when she'd finished, "what is it you want, sweetheart?"

"I don't know," she cried.

"I think you do. I don't think I have to tell you that the Altamira will always be your home if you need or want it," her father said.

"I know." There was a time when his words would have meant everything to her. Right now they only made her sad.

"Let me tell you something," her father said after a moment. "You know that your grandfather started the Altamira. He worked hard to build it up and make it one of the best ranches in Texas. It was his legacy to me and my children."

"I know," she said. It was that pride in her grandfather's legacy along with her love for the ranch that had made her stay after college.

"But, Levi, I never wanted to be a rancher," her father said. "I hated it. I found what I wanted in politics. I want my legacy to you to be freedom. Freedom to be and do whatever your heart desires."

She knew what her heart desired. "I'm sorry, Daddy, that I didn't understand before how you felt about politics," she said. Thanks to Seth Gantry, she now understood passion. "You really need to run for president. You have my support."

"Thank you, Levi." She could hear the emotion in his voice. "You don't know how much that means to me. Levi, do you love this Gantry?"

"Oh, Daddy, with all my heart!"

"Then, honey, I suggest you tell him. If there's one thing I've learned, it's that you have to go after what you want. Don't let foolish pride or fear or anyone keep you from someone you love.''

She smiled through her tears. "I love you, Daddy. I guess you know this means I won't be home for Christmas."

"There'll be other Christmases," her father said. "Tell Gantry— Never mind, I'll tell him when I see him at the wedding. I hope it will be at the Altamira."

She laughed. "There's no place I'd rather be married. But don't you think we should wait until he asks me?"

"The man would have to be a fool not to ask you," McCord said. "And I have a feeling Seth Gantry is no fool. Not if he's fallen in love with my daughter."

She thought of the Altamira. "Daddy, who's going to run the ranch if I don't come back?"

"I have someone in mind," he said slowly. "Someone I think you'll approve of when the time comes."

"Someone who can love it?"

"Yes, Levi. Someone who can love it."

"Thank you, Daddy. I never doubted that you'd make a wonderful president. I just want you to know that."

She cashed in her ticket and rented a car, a four-wheel drive, and headed for the Double Bar G.

SETH WAS IN the living room of the Double Bar G with his family, everyone talking at once, when Levi drove up.

It was his little sister Casey who spotted her rental

car. "Wonder who that could be?" she said, and eyed Seth suspiciously.

Seth glanced out to see Levi step from the car. It was all he could do not to run. His face split in the biggest grin of his life as he rushed out the door and met her before she could get up the porch steps.

She smiled. That was all it took. That wondrous, lift-you-off-your-feet smile of hers. He didn't need to ask how she felt about him or about them. The answer was in that smile, in that expressive face. She'd never been able to hide anything from him. Especially her love.

He swept her off her feet and swung her around in his good arm with a whoop that echoed across the countryside. Then he put her down and looked into her violet eyes. Snowflakes fell around them, white, icy lace.

Seth leaned down to kiss her, to claim her, to seal their love. Her kiss answered his promises with promises of her own. She filled him with such love for her, he thought he'd burst with the happiness of it.

"Aren't you even going to introduce her?" Casey said behind him.

He lifted his lips from Levi's and looked into her eyes, promising her he would finish this later. Slipping his arm around her, he said, "Levi, I'd like you—" He stopped when he turned to find his entire family on the porch, Casey right in front. "—to meet my family," he finished, laughing. "Gantry family, this is Olivia 'Levi' McCord, the lady who is going to be my wife. That is, if she'll have me."

He looked over at Levi. "Will you marry me?"

Her eyes turned a soft lavender. Snow kissed her

cheeks and caught in her lashes as she looked lovingly up at him. "Oh, yes, Seth Gantry. I would love to marry you."

A cheer went up from the porch, and Levi and Seth were swept up by the Gantry clan, everyone laughing and talking at once. Levi would fit in just fine, he thought as he watched his boisterous family surround her.

Seth stood for a moment, the snow falling all around him, listening to the sound of home. It was wondrous. Just like the woman he'd brought to it.

He took Levi's hand and together they walked up the steps.

Get ready for heart-pounding romance and white-knuckle suspense!

HARLEQUIN®

I N T R I G U E®

raises the stakes in a new miniseries

THE McCORD **FAMILY** COUNTDOWN

The McCord family of Texas is in a desperate race against time!

With a killer on the loose and the clock ticking toward midnight, a daughter will indulge in her passion for her bodyguard; a son will come to terms with his past and help a woman with amnesia find hers; an outsider will do anything to save his unborn child and the woman he loves.

With time as the enemy, only love can save them!

#533 STOLEN MOMENTS
B.J. Daniels
October 1999

#537 MEMORIES AT MIDNIGHT
Joanna Wayne
November 1999

#541 EACH PRECIOUS HOUR
Gayle Wilson
December 1999

Available at your favorite retail outlet.

HARLEQUIN®
Makes any time special ™

Visit us at www.romance.net

HICD

Looking For More Romance?

Visit Romance.net

Look us up on-line at: http://www.romance.net

Check in daily for these and other exciting features:

Hot off the press

View all current titles, and purchase them on-line.

What do the stars have in store for you?

Horoscope

Hot deals

Exclusive offers available only at Romance.net

Plus, don't miss our interactive quizzes, contests and bonus gifts.

PWEB

"This book is DYNAMITE!"
—**Kristine Rolofson**

"A riveting page turner..."
—**Joan Elliott Pickart**

"Enough twists and turns to keep everyone
guessing... What a ride!"
—**Jule McBride**

See what all your favorite authors
are talking about.

Coming October 1999 to a retail store near you.

HARLEQUIN®
Makes any time special ™

Look us up on-line at: http://www.romance.net   PHQ4993

Makes any time special ™

WIN A DREAM

In celebration of Harlequin®'s golden anniversary

Enter to win a *dream!* You could win:

- A luxurious trip for two to *The Renaissance Cottonwoods Resort* in Scottsdale, Arizona, or

- A bouquet of flowers once a week for a year from **FTD**, or

- A $500 shopping spree, or

- A fabulous bath & body gift basket, including **K-tel**'s *Candlelight and Romance* 5-CD set.

Look for **WIN A DREAM** flash on specially marked Harlequin® titles by Penny Jordan, Dallas Schulze, Anne Stuart and Kristine Rolofson in October 1999*.

FTD

RENAISSANCE.
COTTONWOODS RESORT
SCOTTSDALE, ARIZONA

K·TEL

*No purchase necessary—for contest details send a self-addressed envelope to Harlequin Makes Any Time Special Contest, P.O. Box 9069, Buffalo, NY, 14269-9069 (include contest name on self-addressed envelope). Contest ends December 31, 1999. Open to U.S. and Canadian residents who are 18 or over. Void where prohibited.

PHMATS-GR

HARLEQUIN®

I N T R I G U E ®

proudly presents a new series from Kelsey Roberts, award-winning author of *The Rose Tattoo* books.

Tough. Rugged. Sexy as sin.

Seven brothers, Montana born and bred, raised in the shadows of the Rocky Mountains and a family secret. Ranchers at heart, protectors by instinct—lovers for keeps.

October 1999
#535 HIS ONLY SON

January 2000
#545 LANDRY'S LAW

June 2000
#565 BEDSIDE MANNER

Watch for all seven *Landry Brothers* books— only from Kelsey Roberts and Harlequin Intrigue!

Available at your favorite retail outlet.

HARLEQUIN®
Makes any time special ™

Visit us at www.romance.net

HILAND

Amnesia...
an unknown danger...
a burning desire.

With

HARLEQUIN®

I N T R I G U E®

you're just

A MEMORY AWAY

from passion, danger...and love!

**Look for all the books in this
exciting miniseries:**

**#527 ONE TEXAS NIGHT
by Sylvie Kurtz**
August 1999

**#531 TO SAVE HIS BABY
by Judi Lind**
September 1999

**#536 UNDERCOVER DAD
by Charlotte Douglas**
October 1999

A MEMORY AWAY—where remembering
the truth becomes a matter of life,
death...and love!

Available wherever Harlequin books are sold.

HARLEQUIN®
Makes any time special ™

Look us up on-line at: http://www.romance.net   HIAMA2

HARLEQUIN®

I N T R I G U E®

43
Light St.

Outside, it looks like a
charming old building
near the Baltimore
waterfront, but inside
lurks danger...
and romance.

"First lady of suspense"
Ruth Glick writing as
Rebecca York returns with

#534 MIDNIGHT CALLER
October 1999

Meg Faulker awakened with no memory of
her accident, no memory of who she was or
why she'd infiltrated Glenn Bridgman's
isolated compound. Was she the beautiful spy
he expected? And more important, was he her
protector—or her captor?

Available at your favorite retail outlet.

HARLEQUIN®
Makes any time special ™

Look us up on-line at: http://www.romance.net   HI43

COMING NEXT MONTH

#537 MEMORIES AT MIDNIGHT by Joanna Wayne
The McCord Family Countdown

Darlene Remington couldn't remember who wanted her dead, but she recognized Sheriff Clint Richards easily—she'd walked away from his strong, protective arms six years ago. Seeing Darlene again reminded Clint just how much he needed a woman in his life— Darlene, to be specific. In a race to find her would-be killer, was Clint ready to confront his past...and willing to risk his heart?

#538 NO BABY BUT MINE by Carly Bishop

Thrown together by tragedy, Kirsten McCourt and Garrett Weisz had shared one night of compassion—and pleasure. Five years later, caught in the grasp of a powerful vigilante leader, Kirsten and Garrett are reunited by danger. Determined to keep Kirsten safe and in his life, Garrett will stop at nothing to obtain justice—especially when he finds that her kidnapped son is also his....

#539 FOR HIS DAUGHTER by Dani Sinclair

Accused of his ex-wife's murder, with no memory of the night in question, Officer Lee Garvey turned to Kayla Coughlin for help. Kayla had never trusted the police, but Lee's obvious devotion to his two-year-old daughter made it difficult to believe the man could be capable of murder—and their mutual attraction made him hard to resist....

#540 WHEN NIGHT DRAWS NEAR by Lisa Bingham

When their plane makes an emergency landing in the snowy wilderness of the Rocky Mountains, Elizabeth Boothe and Seth Brody must fight against an unknown killer and the still-smoldering attraction of their failed marriage. Stranded, with only each other to trust, the couple must overcome both danger and desire to make it off the mountain alive....

Look us up on-line at: http://www.romance.net